Stay conner

Joshua Tree

by

Joshua Perez

the Peppertree Press
Sarasota, Florida

Graphic design by Rebecca Barbier.

For information regarding permission,
call 941-922-2662 or contact us at our website:
www.peppertreepublishing.com or write to:
the Peppertree Press, LLC.
Attention: Publisher
1269 First Street, Suite 7
Sarasota, Florida 34236

ISBN: 978-1-61493-461-5

Library of Congress Number: 2016913058

Printed September 2016

Dedications

To my dog, Nina Perez, thank you for licking my lips that one time. It was kind of gross, but cute. I would prefer you to not do that though, just putting that out there.

To my WHOLE family, no you're not in this book so don't ask ...oh, and thanks for being awesome and getting my book. I appreciate that. If you don't like it...you're dead to me. I'm kidding. I would prefer you to not talk to me though, and avoid eye contact when around me. Love you all!

Prologue

H*er eyes were the last things I saw as I died.* They were a beautiful, yet unnatural, glowing shade of gray. They were different from the ones I've known for almost my whole life. They used to be light and warm, filled with life … they were beautiful. I remember how they would complement her smile. Like how a blanket complemented a bed, making it warm and cozy. How her eyes would slightly wrinkle on the sides when she smiled.

How they used to stare at me, making my feelings for her grow so much stronger … they almost seemed tangible, but fragile. She would look at me, and I would hold my feelings in my hands, plain enough for everyone to see. But I would never be able to hand them to her, because if she didn't accept them, they would fall … shatter … leaving me broken.

So many things have changed now. She has changed and so have her eyes … literally. They're an unfamiliar, unnatural, ice-cold gray now—yet still beautiful. Her eyes were so unreal, yet the more blood I lost—the softer and slower my breath got—the more real they seemed to look.

Shit, I think I've lost too much blood, because honestly, I'm not sure any of that made *any* sense. I'm also being a bit too poetic here, aren't I? I guess this is how somebody thinks when they're dying … ? But I am just being a boy melting over a girl, because I'm dying, OK—totally not being overdramatic here.

This moment felt extremely wrong though. She had so much emotion in her eyes as she held the knife inside me. Even a small tear fell gently down her unnaturally pale face. Why the tear?

Regret, I realized, thinking to myself. She didn't want to do this, and yet she firmly held the knife, stabbing me just below my heart, hitting a lung I think. I started to feel the pain—it hurt *so* much. It felt like more than a body wound interestingly though. It felt like this knife was piercing my … *soul.* Again, maybe I'm not thinking straight. I need to stop thinking about the knife. OK, back to her face!

So pale, it definitely was not human the way she looked, or at least not like a living human. She would not show any emotion across her face anymore, not since she changed. I still remember her before she changed though. The way her nose would slightly wrinkle when she smiled. Sometimes when she laughed hard enough, she would slightly snort, which was possibly the cutest thing you could *ever* hear. Thinking about it brought tears to my eyes.

We stood so close to each other, and this moment felt so intimate. I would really have enjoyed this moment more … if, you know … she didn't have a knife plunged through my ribs. We have known each other so long, yet this wasn't the same girl I talked to about life and our dreams for the future. She has changed, yet so have I.

"I'm sorry," her mouth barely whispered. I heard the emotions from her, but I could barely see them in her face. Her pale face was straight and emotionless, like a beautiful ice sculpture. Her eyes were where all the emotions lay, that's why they locked me in their stare.

I attempted to say, "*It's OK,*" but I kind of just sputtered—can't really blame me. Some blood fell down my chin. Lord, I probably looked gross right now. Why was this OK though? Why could I so easily forgive the person that was killing me? Well, I guess the answer to these questions is pretty easy and painfully obvious to you by now.

I love her—just a boy in love with a girl. I've felt this way about her for years and never knew if she felt the same. Probably not, considering I was dying by her hand. What would be the point of dying with hate though—right? She pulled the knife out.

My brain did not agree with the amount of blood loss that came after that. My head swam and I fell forward as she caught me. She threw the knife away and I glanced at it as it clattered to the ground. It looked like a regular knife, with a black wooden handle. Except that it had some strange markings on the handle and on the flat part of the knife, which was covered in my blood now. *What a cool knife,* I thought to myself, my head feeling woozy, like I was drunk. *At least I got killed by a cool knife.*

She slowly brought me down onto the road, now slightly wet with my blood, too. She slowly flipped me over on my back, holding my head up. She was so careful with me. I was probably looking as pale as she was at this point, although, I know I *definitely* didn't look as great. I felt myself uncontrollably shaking a bit, I was so cold. It's strange, the moment you realize you're actually going to die …

"I'm so sorry," she whispered again, "I wish it didn't have to be like this …"

I didn't even have a chance to attempt to respond this time—everything faded away too fast. That's when the weight of life lifted, and I came face-to-face with God once again.

Part 1:

Hate Him

Chapter 1

"Joshua Tree!" Joshua's mom called out trying to wake him up. This was the fourth time she called out his name from the front passenger seat of the van, but Joshua continued to ignore her and pretended to sleep.

10 Years Ago

Why am I ignoring my mom? Well, I didn't want to get up, because I was extremely comfortable in my bed. I call it my "bed," but it really is just a bunch of mats in my section of the van in the back. Which, I guess you could call this section my "room" then. OK, so I was comfortable in my room/bed—all right?

Yeah, I live in a van with my mom and dad. We live like nomads you could say, moving from place-to-place—don't judge. We've been to a lot of states in America, which is kind of cool. I'm not sure if it's all of them, but I would say we've definitely been to most of them. I'm only nine years old and I've probably been to more states than you have.

Every once in a while, my parents would be able to pay for us to sleep in a motel, but that happened rarely. I'll admit sleeping in a motel was a treat, because the beds would be more comfortable than my mats in our van.

Sometimes there was a TV in the room, too, which I rarely got to watch, because, again—that happened *rarely*. The only thing I had for entertainment in the van was the radio. To be honest though, I'm not really sure where my parents got money for us to pay for gas or anything else we needed to live—like food, for example.

We ate extremely cheap stuff—even dinners—that consisted of things from the dollar store. I know what you're thinking … "Yum!" But, yeah, I mean, we get by. I never knew why we lived this lifestyle, but it's just how we lived ever since I was born, so I never really questioned it.

My parents are kind of hippie-like though, too. I could definitely see them in the 70s. The way we lived would possibly make a little more sense, if it were the 70s. We even have a small peace sign on the front of our black and green van, but it's not the 70s. So I guess we just look like hobos living in a van. My parents do say our last name is "Tree" though. How can you get any more hippie-like than that? I'm pretty sure that is not our legal last name, but to be honest, I do like it, so … I don't care.

You could also say that we're spiritual people—feeling like we're connected to the world and nature and what-not, but I still don't think living in a van was done completely by choice—or at least, by any *good* choices.

After calling my name for the seventh time, my mom finally just got up, crawled over the passenger seat and started shaking me.

"Ugh, I'm up. I'm up!" I said, sitting up and throwing off my blanket with frustration. "Mom, it is way too early … or late—or whatever time it is—for me to be up."

"Oh, give me a break! The sun is coming up in an hour or so. You are nine years old; practically a man," she said, turning on the light on the ceiling of the van. The light was a soft yellow and wasn't that bright, but I still didn't enjoy it ridding me of my peaceful darkness.

"Obviously," I said sarcastically, in between a yawn and rubbing my eyes. They adjusted to the light and I looked at my mom, trying to seem annoyed. She just smiled at me and looked back at me with those pretty brown eyes. She always smiled at me, which made me even more annoyed. I grunted back at her happiness.

"OK, sleepyhead," she chuckled, and kissed my forehead, her long-brown hair lightly touching my cheeks. "Get your boots on and help me to collect some sticks for the fire for breakfast later."

"Fine!"

"Don't give me attitude."

"Fine," I said, with "less attitude," grabbing my boots as instructed right across from me. I looked in the driver seat where I'm used to seeing Dad, noticing it was empty.

"Hey, Mom, where's Dad at?" I asked, even though I kind of already knew what the answer would be.

She hesitated, "Oh ... he's out … doing business."

Ah, and there it was, the famous "doing business" saying. I was used to hearing this answer every time I asked. For years, my dad would disappear to go do "business" and I always wondered what he was out doing. Any time I would question my dad or mom about what he was out doing, they would avoid giving me a straight answer.

They used to say he was out going to the bathroom—of course, and I bought that for a long time when I was little. Then his disappearances seemed too frequent, and he would be out for a while. I don't think anybody takes that long to go to the bathroom.

He would also bring his backpack with him, never letting me look inside it. I used to imagine that he was a secret agent or a super hero … or maybe even a super-hero agent! Probably hiding his amazing super suit and equipment in that bag!

… OK, unlikely I know, but my mom always seemed kind of nervous when he was out. So I figured it must be something kind of dangerous. I'd like to imagine him being a hero of some kind. Kid can dream, can't he?

"Right, business" I said, clearly unconvinced, but she ignored my suspicious tone and me. She handed me my black jacket and slipped on hers, waited for me to slip on my jacket and my boots, and then turned off the light, opening the two big doors at the end of the van, letting in the Ohio cold.

Chapter 2

The van's doors opened up revealing the dark, cold forest outside. Joshua stared out into the dark forest, hungry ... for food.

My stomach growled. Man, I would like a taco or something for breakfast—haven't had one of those in a while. Tacos are so delicious.

Anyways, to keep this story rolling—yeah, we had driven into the middle of a forest in Ohio and parked here for the night. I'm not good at keeping track of the seasons, but I think we were near the end of winter, so it was still pretty cold. I hate the cold, especially when I was so warm before under my blanket.

My mom handed me a small flashlight, because it was still dark out in the forest, and stepped outside the van, her boots crunching on some snow on the ground. She then turned on her own flashlight, revealing the creepy forest in front of her.

I'll admit it, it was kind of creepy being out in the middle of the woods at night—I would have preferred waiting in the van until the sun came up. My mom turned and noticed I was still sitting in the van. She looked at me with the "you-better-stop-fooling-around-and-get-out-here" face. Yeah, it's a specific face that only I could interpret. I looked at her with my "I'm-coming-relax-just-give-me-a-moment-to-adjust-to-this-creepy-forest-around-us" face.

I sighed and stepped out of our van, the cold causing my cheeks to tingle, the slushy-snowy ground crunching under my boots as I stepped down. The ground was slightly covered by snow, but it was only a thin layer. I clicked my flashlight on and looked around me. All I saw were trees, bushes, and more slushy-snow.

I looked up at the sky and could tell it was going to be a cloudy day. It was still dark, but the sky was a slightly brighter gray, so I could tell the sun was on its way.

"All right, Joshua," my mom said looking at me, the cold air making her breath visible, "I'm going to head in the direction your dad went just to make sure he's OK. You stay around here and collect some sticks. Don't walk too far, OK? Not sure what animals could be out here, so don't go too far from the van."

"Can't I just go with … "

"No, honey," she said cutting me off, "we've been over this and you're not allowed to follow Dad when he goes to do his business."

"I don't understand," I said, slightly frustrated, "why can't you guys tell me what he's out doing all the time?"

"Honey, it's just safer for you not to know," she said.

Safer? I never heard her put it that way before, I thought to myself. *Why do they fight me on this so much?* I never liked them keeping this stuff from me. There wasn't much we kept from each other. I mean, we lived with each other and were around each other 24/7 for God's sake, there wasn't much to keep secret—except this apparently.

"I'm pretty sure Dad doesn't want *you* following him though, and you normally don't go," I argued, "so you shouldn't go either."

"Joshua," she said slightly annoyed, "I'm not arguing with you on this. Now go pick up some sticks and meet me back here. Be careful and don't go far, OK?"

I was annoyed, so I didn't respond. I just stepped past her and started walking through the dark woods. I could tell she didn't like how I just walked away from her, but she decided not to push the argument any further and walked the opposite way—the way Dad had gone, I'm guessing.

That kid got that attitude from me, I swear, Jean thought to herself as her son, Joshua, angrily walked away from her through the dark woods.

I sighed, then shined my flashlight in front of me and started walking in the direction I had seen my husband, Brandon, going earlier. We've been living this life for a long time and Brandon's "business" was dangerous. Meeting up with what I felt were unstable people—my nice way for describing drug addicts—and, honestly, doing the exact opposite of helping them.

I never wanted to live this life exactly, but ever since Brandon almost lost his life about ten years ago and my parents abandoned us, things have been tough. Both Brandon and I never went to college, so getting decent jobs was hard, and paying for a house was difficult too. We had made so many wrong decisions. Honestly I knew we were basically failing life to put it bluntly, but I couldn't give up. I felt the world had something in store for our family.

I felt that my greatest gift was Joshua, and the world had something in store for him, even though we as parents have been failing him. This may not have been an ideal way to raise a kid, but a part of me liked living on the road. I know it's not exactly a stable life for my son and none of this was ever done on purpose, but I felt we were close as a family and we felt connected to the world.

Snow crunched under my boots as I walked looking for my husband. Cool air flowed over my face, causing my cheeks to tingle. Being outside in nature, feeling free just felt … right.

I stopped and touched a tree, closing my eyes, feeling the cool ice-cold bark, and took a deep breath of the cold air.

Yeah, I thought to myself, *this just feels right.* I enjoyed just taking moments like this, feeling the connection to the world. I opened my eyes, taking my hand off the tree, and continued walking through the cold snowy forest.

I usually left Brandon alone when he went to go make deals, but today was different. I knew I was fighting fate, but now that the day Brandon was going to die was here, I felt I had no choice, but to fight it. I had made a mistake ten years ago to save his life from cancer. I wanted to do whatever I could to fix my mistake, and save my husband's life again.

Chapter 3

I guess I feel kind of bad giving my mom attitude, Joshua Tree thought as he continued walking around the forest, searching for firewood.

I'll apologize to her later.

The sun slowly made its way up, but I was right. It was another cold, gray day. I put the bundle of sticks I had found down onto the snowy ground, so that I could switch my flashlight off. It was bright enough to see now, so I slipped the small flashlight into my back pocket.

I got ready to pick up my sticks again when I noticed a pretty awesome stick stuck in the ground not far from me. It was bigger than all of the ones I found so far, about the size of my arm. I went and pulled it out of the ground. I waved it around pretending it was a sword and I was a hero defending the world from every evil being that got in my way.

I wanted to follow my mom, but at the same time, I did enjoy playing by myself. I was *always* with my parents. I started using the stick to hit a tree pretending it was a bad guy.

At first, I was just playing, and then I started to feel myself actually growing angry. What was I angry at? Maybe my parents and their secret keeping … maybe that I didn't have any friends … I had no one to talk to except my parents. But sometimes it was them I was mad at, so who could I talk to about that? No one.

I hit the tree harder and harder. The bark slightly started to dent from my hits, small bits of bark chipping off. I stopped, breathing hard, my breath visible from the cold. I felt a bit better, since I let out some of the frustration. I noticed the marks on the tree from my blows. Something inside me felt like what I just did was wrong. I threw the stick away and stepped up to the tree, put my hand against the cool bark, closed my eyes and took a deep breath of the cold …

Pow! Pow! I jumped down on the ground, into the freezing snow, hearing some animals run away in fear of … whatever those loud sounds were. I lay there on the ground for a minute, breathing really hard. Just staring at the snow mixed with dirt under me scared of whatever was going on. Were those gunshots though? I've only ever heard them on TV, but that sounded so much louder and scarier, more real. Where could they be coming from?

"BRANDON!!" I heard a woman yell in the distance. That was my dad's name and I was pretty sure that was my mom's voice, but she sounded so scared and I never heard her scream like that.

I got up on my feet, slightly wet from the snow, and ran back towards the van as fast as I could. Running past the van, I ran the direction I had seen my mom go after my dad.

"MOM? DAD? Is everything OK?" I yelled, with my teeth chattering, still sprinting. The wind was causing me to shiver since I was wet now. I didn't hear anything as I kept running. "MOM! DAD!" I yelled again. This time I heard a response.

"Stay back, Joshua!" my mom yelled. I finally saw her in the distance. When I got closer, I was so shocked I stopped running in my tracks, staring at the scene in front of me. She was on her knees holding my dad in her arms. He had bullet holes in his chest with blood oozing out of them. I only saw the back of his head, because my mom was grasping his head in her chest with her fingers entwined in his dark black hair. There was a halo of blood all around my parents, accented against the white snow.

"Mommy … no … " I didn't even know what to say, I was in such shock. "Is Dad OK?…" I started to ask, when I heard a "*click*." I was so distracted by my parents, I hadn't noticed a man slowly walking towards me with a gun. He aimed the gun at me in his shaking hand and my dad's backpack in his other hand.

He was kind of tall and had a bald head with a really thick, dark-brown beard. The strangest thing was his eyes though. They were blood-shot, and his irises were …

OK, now this is going to sound crazy … but his irises were changing from black to white …to green. It made no sense and I thought maybe my mind was playing tricks on me. But the more I stared at him, I could clearly see … his irises were actually changing color. Chills ran down my spine. I put my hands out in front of me as if to try and keep this man away.

"Your dad is a bastard, kid," he said with a rough voice, "these are all I have!!" he yelled lifting my dad's backpack toward me. A few baggies fell out of it onto ground. I looked at my dying dad in my mom's arms and back at this crazy man with strange eyes. I finally realized what was going on and I felt ashamed and sad.

This was how they made money. All of a sudden, it made sense. I thought of my dad as a hero and now I was … disappointed.

"These drugs are shit, kid!" he yelled, throwing the whole backpack full of drugs onto the ground. "The voices are still here! These damn demons … angels … in my head! They won't go away…GET OUT OF ME! I DON'T WANT TO KILL ANYONE!" he yelled while staring at me, his face contorted in what looked like pain. He almost looked like he was pleading for help. This man didn't make much sense, but I assumed he wouldn't. He did not look like a man who was thinking straight.

I started to panic more as he continued to try and aim his gun at me. *RUN!* something inside me said, but I couldn't think straight, plus my parents were right there, so I couldn't just leave them.

I couldn't control my breathing as it rapidly sped up, condensation streaming out of my mouth. The man was struggling just to keep his hand from shaking, trying to keep the gun straight. I glanced over at my mom who was panicking too, but her attention wasn't on me. She was trying to stop my dad from bleeding using his own shirt. I wanted her to come help me, because the seriousness of the situation was really beginning to scare me, but she was clearly having a panic attack and wasn't thinking straight. I didn't know what to do, but I needed to do *something.*

"Please," I managed finally to force myself to say looking back at the crazy man. I realized I was crying. "I'll do whatever I can to help you."

He shot me.

The pain was overwhelming. I'm not sure if he did it on purpose, or if he just couldn't aim correctly, but he got me in my left thigh. I fell to the ground.

There was so much pain, I'm not sure how long I laid there, grasping my leg to my chest. I opened my eyes, but the world was a blurr, because of all the tears streaming out of them. The man stood there—just stood there—and stared at me. His irises were black now, accented by his blood-shot eyes, like a drop of black ink in the middle of blood. His eyes held no emotion and he just stared at me with his arms at his sides now, the gun on the ground.

Something finally seemed to click in his mind and he just ran away. I looked at my mom and she was dragging my dad's limp body towards me, leaving behind her a trail of blood in the snow.

"Joshua … I'm so sorry … this wasn't supposed to happen," she gasped as she struggled to drag my dad's body towards me, "I'll get the phone in the van. I'll get help!" She laid my dad a few feet away from me and then sprinted off towards the van, leaving us lying on the ground. I felt something warm on my cheek as I lay on the ground—my own blood. The pain was finally too much, so the world started to get fuzzy.

It's strange, the moment you realize you're actually going to die … the world faded into blackness.

Chapter 4

"CLEAR!!" the doctor yelled as he put the defibrillator onto Brandon's bloody chest. They were in a battle for his life … and they were losing. Jean stood just outside the emergency door in the hallway, staring at the battle for her husband's life, her cheeks wet from tears.

One of the assistants noticed that the door to the emergency room was open and saw me looking in. She looked at me almost as if to say "*I'm sorry,*" and closed the emergency door.

Tears fell down my face as I walked down the hallway. I walked up to a window that looked into the room where my son laid in a bed with his left thigh all bandaged up. He was connected to some machine to help him breathe and a bag of blood. He was sleeping, but looked so pale. It hurt me to see him like this. I couldn't force myself to walk in there and see him any closer, because this was my fault.

A doctor walked up next to me as I was looking at my son. He tried to touch my shoulder, but I flinched away slightly. I didn't want him to do that—that was a sign of condolence and I didn't want that right now. "Please don't say it. He has to be fine," I said.

"Ms. Rodriguez … " the doctor started.

"Tree, my last name is Tree." I said interrupting him. I heard him talking to my parents over the phone just a few minutes ago. I'm sure they told him our whole situation and how crazy I am about "changing" my last name to Tree. They don't understand how important it was to us. He sighed.

"Mrs. Tree," he said slowly, "we're not sure if your … husband is going to make it. We have the best doctors working on saving him at this moment, but … " he paused, probably trying to think of how to say it.

"He's not going to make it," I said helping him out, "I know."

"Yes." He said, slightly unsettled by my response, but I didn't care. Then I gestured toward my son, Joshua.

"What about Joshua? Why does he look so bad? It was only his leg."

"He, unfortunately, might not make it either." The doctor said. I looked at him in shock.

"What? Please … not both … it was just his leg … " Fresh tears started falling down my face. It felt like these tears would never stop. *How could I lose both of them? This can't happen. This wasn't supposed to happen.*

"Joshua's body is struggling with working on its own because of the dramatic blood loss. If he would have gotten here quicker, and we were able to give his body blood sooner, his situation wouldn't be as bad. But since it took so long … "

He paused and sighed again—which was getting on my nerves a bit, to be honest—then continued, "his body has started shutting down. We're just unsure if … "

I couldn't listen to him anymore and walked quickly away. I heard him call out my name behind me, but I started running. I couldn't just stand there and watch my husband and son die in front of me, I had to do something and I couldn't do it here. I had to fix this. I ran out of the hospital.

Joshua Tree woke up in a hospital bed, noticing his left thigh was all bandaged up. Then, looking up, noticing that there was an older lady sitting near the door of his hospital room reading a book.

She looked kind of like my mom, but a lot older. She also had tanner skin than my mom, with some gray mixed in with her short, dark-brown hair. When she saw I was awake, she seemed surprised, closing her book and putting it down on the small table next to her.

"Hi, Joshua," she said with a slight Spanish accent, "how are you feeling?"

"Sore, but I'll survive," I replied, trying to move my left leg but it hurt even trying so I gave up. I looked back at this stranger.

"Um…who are you?"

"Oh, of course, sorry." She said seeming kind of nervous, "I'm Melina. I'm actually your grandma, on your mother's side."

My grandma? And I'm half Spanish? I thought. I never met my grandparents before. Honestly, the only people I knew in my life were my parents. Never met other family members or even made friends, we traveled too much for that. My parents never talked about my grandparents either.

"Oh, hi," I said, honestly not sure of how to reply to that. "Are my parents OK?" For a second she looked like she was bit disappointed that I wasn't more excited to meet her, but she hid that right away.

"Oh … yes, they're fine. I'll admit, it's a miracle your dad made it though. When I got here he was in bad shape and Jean, I mean your mom was," she paused, "also not in good shape—emotionally—at least from what the doctors told me. But she seems fine now that you and your father are getting better. She's getting some food from the hospital cafeteria." I felt a sense of relief.

Yeah, it really did seem like a miracle that my dad was still alive. The picture of him in my mom's arms surrounded by blood in the snow flashed in my head again and I shivered.

"How long have I been out?" I asked, trying to get my mind off that horrible scene.

"About three days."

Jeez ... three days I was just laying here? Long time.

"You lost a lot of blood, but you're healing well the doctors told me. Your father is still sleeping, but he's healing, too. The doctors are surprised with how both of you are doing so well all of a sudden. Again, it's miracle." She stood up from her chair and grabbed a water bottle that was next to her book on the small table. She walked towards me and offered it. She smiled, but I could tell she was a bit nervous. I grabbed it and nodding my thanks, took a few sips, and then put it down on the table next to my bed.

She sighed, then walked back to her chair and sat down and said, "Joshua, your grandpa and I have had" she paused, as if trying to think of the right word, "problems in the past with your parents. We knew you guys must have not been living normally when your parents had run off, but we honestly didn't know the extent of your lifestyle."

She said all this carefully, as if cautious not to offend me. "This situation really has changed things and we believe you should definitely not live this way anymore. We've talked to your mom and we have agreed that you and your parents, once all of you are well enough, need to come live with us in Florida and live a more stable life."

She looked at me as if I was about to argue, and honestly I would have. Because strangely, I liked the way we lived. It was all I knew and I didn't want it to change. Then the picture of the man and his strange eyes flashed in my head, his shaking hand with the gun in it.

What was wrong with his eyes? I wanted to talk to someone about that, but I'd probably sound crazy.

Either way, I knew now that we weren't safe the way we were living. Things had to change and I was just beginning to realize that. What happened had changed everything anyway—I had to face that. We might as well try and be a bit safer. I sighed and just said, "OK." I knew there was no point in fighting and decided just to give in to the change. I could tell my grandma was relieved that I didn't fight. All I could do was hope life could only get better from here.

Chapter 5

10 Years Later

His eyes held no emotion
Only evil
His black irises slowly turned pure white as he smiled
He laughed

Joshua Tree quickly sat up on his bed, breathing rapidly. He looked around as if he was being watched, but quickly seemed to realize he was just dreaming.

Why are these dreams happening more frequently? I thought, putting my face in my hands. Both my hands and face were slightly wet from sweat. I felt as scared as I did that horrible day. I had a lot of nightmares after what happened to me when I was nine, but around twelve the nightmares slowed down. So for about seven years the dreams were generally gone. Lately, they have been rapidly coming back though—and different. More intense, and those white eyes …

BEEP! BEEP! BEEP! I jumped up off my bed and fell onto my stomach on the floor. Quickly realizing it was just my alarm, I stood up on my feet and hit the Off button. The nightmares caused me to wake up right before my alarm. I walked over to my closet to grab my clothes and start changing into them for school, simple T-shirt and shorts. *Great,* I thought as I got dressed, *another day of college.*

When I was nine years old, I had been living in a van with my parents ever since I was born, so I had missed grades 1 to 3. Luckily, once my parents and I started living with my grandparents, they got me back on track using online classes. Took a lot of work, but yeah, nineteen now and I'm in community college.

Once I was dressed, I grabbed my keys off my dresser, putting them in my pocket. Then I went to the bathroom across from my room to brush my teeth and comb my hair. After that, I went back to my room, grabbing my backpack, and headed to the kitchen where I found my grandparents eating their breakfast at the table.

"Good morning," I said to both of them.

"Good morning," they both said, basically at the same time. My grandpa looked up from his eggs and said with his deep, Hispanic-accented voice, "I worked on your van. It should hopefully be running better." I felt bad having him work on the van. Honestly, he wasn't getting any younger—his hair, gray and thinning, and his tan skin wrinkling.

I felt that I should be doing the hard work, but honestly, I would be making the van worse, if I got my hands on it. I also didn't have a job to pay for anyone else to fix it yet.

"Thanks a lot, Grandpa." I said, walking over and shaking his hand. My grandpa liked shaking hands. I'm not sure why, but it felt like it replaced giving him hugs.

My grandma looked at me and she had her "something-is-wrong-with-Joshua-so-I-need-to-stare-awkwardly-at-him-and-figure-it-out" face, so I waited as she analyzed me.

"Did you take a shower? I didn't hear the shower," she said. I stared at her as she waited for me to reply. I knew she was just trying to be helpful, but it always felt like she was slightly insulting me.

"I took a shower last night, Grandma, so I smell fine and clean. Have my parents left for work?" I asked, changing the subject away from my body odor. They both nodded.

My parents both had jobs, so they could help my grandparents with paying for things. Grandpa still had a side job helping with fixing cars, but I think he was on the verge of retiring. Grandma was retired from her old job as a lawyer. Yep, my grandma worked as a lawyer for a while. Pretty cool, and apparently she was really amazing at it from what I heard, but she has been retired for a while now.

The reason it took so long for my parents and I to afford living on our own was because both my parents only had a GED. They dropped out of college years ago and lived with my grandparents. Apparently, there was a fight and they got kicked out all those years ago. Then I was born, and nine years later there was that tragedy … so now here we are, living with them again.

My mom had a job as a waitress at a small diner; probably had the breakfast shift, so that's why she left kind of early today. My dad worked at some kind of business. I never can remember what the business is, but I know he gets a lot of calls or something. He is *always* complaining about the calls.

I grabbed a breakfast bar and started to head out. "All right, see you guys later." I said, walking away. My grandma looked up quickly again.

"Wait," she said. I stopped and turned to look at her. *What could possibly be wrong with me now?*

"Kiss," she said.

Oh, right. My grandpa likes to have less affectionate contact as possible, while my grandma likes as much affection as possible.

They're weird.

I gave her a quick kiss on the cheek and walked out of the kitchen. I grabbed my keys out of my pocket, opened the front door, and walked outside.

"Lock the door for me, guys, thanks!" I yelled, closing the door. I walked out towards the old van. Yep, I drove our old home. It was a black and green van with a peace sign on the bumper in the front. This junk van definitely helped me get all the ladies.

Both my parents used my grandparent's old cars and I had this piece of junk—there was a lot of sarcasm when I said it got me the ladies, if you didn't catch that. I loved this van, since it's where I lived for the first nine years of my life, but it really was a piece of junk. I walked to it, opened the front door and sat down on the seat. I put the key into the ignition and twisted it.

tick tick tick tick tick

"Oh please no, don't do this to me you stupid piece of … " I tried to twist the key again harder.

tick tick tick tick tick

"Damn it!" I yelled at the van, hitting the wheel with frustration, but giving up.

I guess my grandpa might be losing his touch. I really didn't feel like going back inside to deliver this bad news yet. An idea popped into my head.

Well, maybe this could be a good excuse to call and maybe see her, I realized, grabbing my cell phone and scrolling down to Kate's name. I pressed her name to call her. She picked up after a few rings, which surprised me.

"Hey, Tree! What's up?" she asked. Ah, yes, she calls me, 'Tree.'

I had told her about my parents and how I went by that last name years ago when I first met her. So now, she just likes to use it as my nickname, which is cool with me.

I found out that my real last name would be Jones, because that is my dad's last name. So they decided to make my last name that legally. My mom's last name is Rodriguez. They never were married legally, but when we used to live on our own on the road, they had just decided to say our last names were 'Tree.' So now, legally, we decided I'd go by Joshua Jones, but in my heart, I was a Tree—sounds funny when I think about it like that.

"Hey, Kate, sorry for the random call, but I'm having van problems again—think I could get a ride to school?" I asked, hopeful.

"Oh, yeah, it's no problem. I'll be there in a few minutes," she replied.

"OK, cool, thanks. See ya."

"See ya," she said, hanging up. I felt slight butterflies in my stomach. I always felt those anytime it actually worked out to where I could hang out with Kate. She didn't live that far away, so it only took about five minutes until she was driving up to my driveway in her blue car.

"Hey, Tree!" she said, as I opened the door and sat down in her passenger seat, throwing my backpack into the back seat.

Gosh, I just loved hearing her voice and seeing her in person, with her brown hair and light-brown eyes. I would say I've always known I felt something for her—problem is the feelings have become stronger as we've gotten older. The reason this becomes a problem is it seems her feelings haven't developed like mine have.

I guess I can't blame her though—I wouldn't say I'm the best-looking guy around. I'm no Prince Charming. I sometimes try and force myself just to stop looking at her that way. But then, I see her eyes, hear her voice, and I'm caught in the trap again. It's an endless circle that I'm not sure will ever end.

Jesus, sometimes I feel like I sound like "Twilight" or some crap when I think about her. This isn't that, I promise … just … no.

"You really have to get that van fixed, Tree, or at least get a new car," Kate said, snapping me out of my thoughts.

"Well, my grandpa is the best at what he does, so if he can't fix that piece of junk, I'm honestly not really sure who can. And psh, like I can afford a new car—thanks for the ride though," I said, as she backed out of my driveway and started driving.

"Oh, it's no problem," she replied, "You'd be screwed without me, huh?"

Oh my God, yeah, I wanted to say but I decided to play it cool and just say, "Yep."

The rest of the ride was kind of awkward. Kate and I are pretty close and have known each other for years. I talked to her about everything, but lately it seems she wants more space. I'm not sure if I've been doing anything wrong or if it's just she's busy.

I've wanted to ask her why things have been different, but I wasn't sure how to bring it up. About twenty minutes later, we were driving up to the front of my small community college building, but only have had small talk about school assignments.

"All right, thanks again Kate for the ride," I said, smiling at her. I took my seat belt off and opened the door. I tried getting some kind of eye contact with her, but she just kept her eyes forward.

"Yep," she said, still looking forward. She appeared to be distracted by her thoughts or something, which also seems to happen more often. She really has looked more stressed lately too, but she never wants to talk about it.

"You think we could meet up at the tree later?" I forced myself to ask. When we first met as kids, we were at the park under this huge tree. It was totally random how we found each other there, but we got along great. It became a ritual to just meet up there and talk.

"Tree? Your last name is Tree?" I remember younger Kate Iris saying back when we first met nine years ago when we were little ten-year-olds. *"Well, actually, I think that's pretty cool! It would make sense if our hangout is under this tree, right, Mr. Tree?"* she would say while giggling. She always found it funny that I thought my last name was Tree. But she was my only friend who never found it stupid. She always accepted me for me.

"Yeah, I'm not sure," Kate said, knocking me back into the present, unfortunately. "I might be kind of busy, but if I can, I'll let you know."

"Oh, OK." I said hiding my disappointment, knowing she most likely wouldn't let me know. It used to be a no-brainer to go hang out. Now it I felt like I was asking her to do some kind of chore.

I stepped out of the car door and shut it. I wasn't that surprised though. Lately she has been kind of distant, but it's not like I could argue with her. So you know, whatever—right? People grow up and fall apart. That's life, I guess. I opened the door in the back and grabbed my backpack off the back seat.

Kill him, the voice in Kate's head whispered.

"I'll talk to you later then," Tree said, as he grabbed his backpack from the back seat. I knew he was disappointed, but the voice was getting stronger, so I had to keep our space.

"Bye," I replied, right when he closed the back door. I felt my emotions being pulled. I should have felt bad that I was clearly pushing Tree away … instead I felt anger. I stared at Tree walking away from my car.

I hated him …

Get yourself together, Kate. Tree is your best friend. I thought, reasoning with myself.

No, he's not. Kill him.

The voice in my head whispered to me again, pushing my own thoughts away.

Why do you fight it? This is what you're meant to do. Kill him, God whispered in my head.

Chapter 6

Kill him.

Kill him.

It's what you're here for.

It's why I created you …

Kate shook her head trying to ignore the voice while driving back to her house after dropping Tree off at school. *Please just go away!* she thought, arguing with the voice in her head.

I made you, the voice whispered angrily, now do what you're meant to do.

"Oh, my god, please just stop!" I yelled out loud. I turned on my radio, revving up the music, as if that would make a difference and I could drown it out of my head. The voice seemed to fade away finally though. Knowing it would come back soon, I tried just to focus on driving and the music. It never stayed away for long.

I must really be going crazy, I thought, which is something I thought basically on a daily basis. The voice said the most stupid things. I would never actually kill Tree, but—boy—was it driving me crazy!

I always had this voice in my head ever since I met Tree when we were ten-year-old kids. It started right away, but so low at first, I didn't think much of it. It would always be at the back of my head, whispering how horrible Tree is. It used to be just a small whisper that would tell me to hate him. Now it has evolved into a louder and more violent voice.

At first, it was just, "*hate him*," which eventually turned into, "*kill him*." I thought it might only be a voice in my head, schizophrenia of some sort, but I'm not so sure any more if I'm being honest. The voice was really starting to scare me.

I never understood why, but Tree seemed to have been the one who triggered this voice. But he's my best friend and has always been there for me. Before I met him, I didn't have any real friends. There was one girl who I thought was my best friend, but she literally disappeared without saying goodbye. I never got over how quickly she just left, but I now had Tree as my best friend.

As much as I liked Tree though, the voice started to become so demanding, so powerful that lately, I felt it pulling ever so slightly on my emotions, causing me to be slightly angry towards him for no real reason. It sounds crazy, but I swear I wasn't trying to be mad at him.

I've begun to believe it may not be a disorder anymore. I thought that the voice might even *be* God. Which may seem crazy and an over-exaggeration, but the way it slightly seemed to pull on my emotions really scared me.

What pushed me over to thinking it was God was … well, it came to me in a dream. I saw a man in a white cape and his eyes *glowed* white. I couldn't really make out any details, because behind him also shined a bright light. All he said in the dream was the same thing he always said, "Kill him. Kill him." This being felt powerful and the dream seemed so realistic. It couldn't possibly just be my imagination … right?

But would *He* demand murder? Would *God* really push a person to kill other human beings for him? Maybe I was just overthinking this.

I started driving in the direction of the mall. I needed to distract myself and do a little "shopping." I couldn't actually buy anything, but it never hurt to look.

**

A few hours later—after gawking at clothes I couldn't afford—I parked my car in the driveway, got out, and started walking towards my house. It was the middle of the day, a really nice day. The sun was shining, the sky was blue, and it just felt nice—I just wish I could enjoy it. Lately I just have felt unhappy and like everything I've done is wrong.

I sound like a normal whining teen or something, but having just lost my job recently really didn't help with my mood much. I wish I could tell my mom about it, but … well, let's just say we're not that close, even though it is literally just us living together. I unlocked the door and walked inside my house.

"Mom," I called out, "you home?" I didn't hear any reply and couldn't see anything at first. It was pretty dark in my house, so it took a minute for my eyes to adjust. I took my shoes and socks off and set them aside.

"Mom?" I called out again, this time hearing slight snoring from my left. I looked over and saw my mom passed out on the couch with a bunch of orange pill bottles in front of her on the small coffee table. This actually wasn't a shocking sight for me.

She didn't take these pills for any actual condition, she had an addiction. She had a job as a guard at some 24/7 gas station, working the night shifts. Then when she got home early in the morning, she would basically overdose off pills and pass out for the whole day. It was her process and sadly, I have gotten used to it. I wasn't really sure how to help her. I didn't want her to go to jail or anything. She would also threaten me, if I mentioned rehab.

Your mother is pathetic, God whispered quietly in my head.

Kill her…kill her … she deserves it … .kill her …

Sighing, and trying to push the voice to the back of my head, I went to pick up the bottles that were empty and on the ground, grabbing the half-filled ones from the table. I took a couple out of a pill bottle and swallowed them.

Whatever pills I took never helped with the voice, but they always helped me get drowsy and fall asleep later. Then I took the pill bottles back to the pantry in our kitchen. I had to take them away to make sure she didn't wake up and instantly take more.

After putting them away, I started to walk back to my room, passing by my passed-out mother again, but then felt my phone vibrate. I took it out and looked at it—it was Tree. I was about to read the text, when out of the corner of my eye, I noticed something in my mom's hand that I hadn't noticed at first—probably since it was so dark and my eyes were fully adjusted now. It was about to fall out of her hand since she was passed out.

It was a gun.

Chapter 7

"Hey, darling, where's my sandwich?!" the bald and overweight man yelled from his table in the middle of the diner. "Jeez, bitch, where's my sandwich?" He continued to yell over all the noise of the small, crowded diner. He even started banging his drink on the table, causing some of the beer to splash out from his bottle.

Great, I'm going to have to be the one to clean that up later, Jean thought. She hated this job with all her might. She hated driving here; hated walking in and seeing the dumb white walls; hated the dumb dirty checkered floors; didn't really have any friends at this place; and hated most of the customers.

But I have to keep pushing, I thought to myself. I put up with it all for my son, Joshua, and Brandon. I loved them more than anything. Whatever suffering I went through was worth it, and honestly, I felt I deserved it most of the time.

"I'll be right with you, sir!" I called back as politely as I could through gritted teeth while pouring another customer a refill of water. It was times like these that I missed just being out on the road with my family.

"That's exactly what the other bitch waitress said! Now go get my damn sandwich or I'm not paying for shit!" the man yelled, taking another gulp of his beer.

Trying not to yell at this man to shut his mouth, I served the customers I was supposed to serve, then went storming towards the kitchen in the back to find Jill. She was the waitress who was serving that ball of sunshine today.

"Jill!" I called, walking down the short hallway into the kitchen. I only saw the chef and his cooks. "Do you know where Jill is?" I asked one of the cooks. "A baby is having a fit over his sandwich."

"I think I saw her leave, not sure if she'll be coming back," the nearest cook said to me, then put a plate with a sandwich on the table in front of me "Here's the baby's sandwich though."

Great, I thought, realizing I'd have to serve that jerk. Grabbing the plate, I headed out of the kitchen. I really considered messing with his sandwich while I walked down the short hallway towards the door.

I was about to open the door to the diner, when I realized something odd that made me pause before opening it. It was eerily quiet on the other side. *That's strange,* I thought. It was always noisy here, because of all the customers, and just about a minute ago, it was noisy as hell.

I slowly opened the door and instantly dropped the plate out of shock. The plate shattered and the food splattered onto the ground. The door flew open the rest of the way on its own, slamming into the wall.

In front of me was the most horrible scene I have ever seen in my life. There were dead bodies everywhere and a man with a bald head and a thick brown beard was standing in the middle of the diner with blood slowly dripping off his hands. He looked up at me. His eyes made me want to run, but I was in such shock, I couldn't get my legs to move. His eyes were bloodshot and his irises were black, looking like drops of ink in blood.

He smiled.

"Man, don't you think that test was easy, Joshua? I was worried at first, but once I got into it, probably the easiest test I ever took!" Joshua Tree's 'friend,' Tyler said to him while they walked out of the community college building in the early afternoon.

He was kind of just one of those 'friends' you have just at school. Once I left this place, I would never see him again until I went back to class. He was a nice guy though, seemed outgoing, and was the only one who talked to me in class. Only problem was, I was the opposite of him. I'm not as nice or as outgoing. I just couldn't make myself just tell him to leave me alone.

"Oh, yeah, totally easy," I lied, "I could have done it in my sleep." He laughed while he scratched his short beard. He had a nice beard, even though he was around my age—he couldn't have been a year or so older than me. I wasn't sure, but I wish I could grow a nice beard like that.

Anyway, I don't know why he laughed. I wasn't trying to be funny. I probably actually failed that test. I stopped walking and looked for a place to sit.

"OK, man, I'll see you next time! We probably should work together on that upcoming presentation!" Tyler said while walking away. He seemed a bit too excited about this presentation … what kind of person was he? Who enjoyed stuff like that?

"OK, yeah, sounds good! See ya," I called back. He walked away towards his car. I probably should have asked for a ride from him, but I imagine we'd have a long conversation about nothing but the presentation, because we have nothing else to talk about. I really didn't want to do that, so I hung around for a bit and decided to take my chances with texting Kate.

"*Hey, Kate,*" I texted, "*can I get a ride back home?*" I pressed

Send, and then sat down on a nearby bench. It really was a nice day—sun was shining, blue sky. I felt like it was one of those picture-perfect days, you know? About five minutes later, Kate responded, "*Probably not - sorry. Can you get one of your parents to get you? I am kind of busy here.*"

Disappointed I just texted back "*OK, see you later then. Meet me at the tree later?*" I waited for her to respond, thinking of what to do now. I decided to text my mom. She sometimes got a long break and may have enough time just to take me home.

"*Hey, Mom,*" I texted, "*I just got out of college. I had Kate drive me here cuz the van is being dumb again. She can't drive me back though cuz she's busy, so can I get a ride back home soon? I'm done with class and waiting.*" I pressed Send and waited.

Chapter 8

The man just stood there with blood slowly dripping of his hands and a smile on his face. He had killed everyone in the diner. How he did it without any of them screaming or calling the cops no one could know, and now he had his eyes on Jean.

"You know why I am here." He finally said, staring at me. His voice didn't look like it matched the way he looked at all. He looked like a man who had been taking drugs on a daily basis to put it bluntly, with his skinny face and body. His bloodshot eyes with black irises gave off this feeling that he would kill you without thinking twice, especially at this moment, with his arms covered in blood. Yet his voice was calm and collected, like if we were having a normal conversation, even though we were standing in the middle of so much death.

This was the same man who had tried to kill my husband and son ten years ago. However, this was not really a man—well, the thing inside him was not a man. He was controlled by a demon, a soul collector, and his name was Alastair. Yes, I knew why he was here, although I was in denial. *Has ten years really gone by that fast?* I thought.

"Come," Alastair said, grabbing the fat bald man who was complaining less than two minutes ago from his chair, throwing his corpse onto the ground. It hit with a skin-crawling *thump*, "Sit."

I felt stiff, but I felt I should do what he said. I walked slowly around all the bodies, trying to avoid the puddles of blood, as I made my way towards the table. I struggled not to throw up from the sight of all the blood and corpses around us. A smell was slowly starting to make its way around the room, which made me sick.

Alastair grabbed the chair with his bloody hand and slid the chair back for me to sit in. I hesitated before sitting, honestly fighting the feeling just to run. He stared at me, his face saying, "*If you run I'll kill you in a heartbeat,*" so I stiffly and quickly sat down. He walked to another table, grabbing a chair from it and noisily slid the chair across the bloody floor, then sat across from me with a smug smile.

"You know why I'm here," he repeated, waiting for me to respond, staring at me with those black irises. The scary thing about his eyes ... was they were kind of pretty when you stared at them. It's hard to admit that, but it's true. His irises were mainly black, but they had a mix of gray in them. Then his eyes were a red backdrop to his glowing irises. I felt disgusted thinking about that.

"Yes," I said with a shaky voice. He reached out across the small table with his bloody hand to touch my face, but I flinched and backed away—that amused him.

He put his hand down and said, "Good, then you should remember our situation. It's been, what—twenty years since our first deal? I spared your 'husband,'" he said making air quotes, "from lung cancer and then I spared him, again, from the gunshots, which were supposed to kill him, because of our first deal, by the way. Then your stupid son was there and I *had* to save his life, too. God, you cried so much that day ... pathetic. I'll admit this deal has taken quite a left turn, because of that day in the woods. I had some unwanted guests show up to the party, but I believe things are back to the way they should be."

I knew everything he was talking about, sort of. I had tried to find my husband before Alastair found him in the woods that day, to warn him so that we could run away or at least not meet with him. I was trying to avoid the deal I had made with Alastair ten years before. It didn't work out, and even worse, somehow my son ended up getting shot. So I made *another* deal with him to save both Brandon and Joshua's soul. I don't know why he was talking about this again. I hated thinking about that day, but there was something I didn't fully understand.

"Why … did you shoot my son that day, too? He didn't have to be part of this … " I asked. I knew he wouldn't answer the question, and he didn't. He just stared at me, emotionless, with those horrible, pretty eyes. He moved on, as if I hadn't even said anything.

"You're lucky I don't give a shit that you were there that day, obviously trying to stop me. You wouldn't have been able to. Either way, here we are now and you owe me two souls. Correct?" He seemed so proud of himself, as if this was just a project that was going well. I nodded.

"But you said you wouldn't kill them. You just would own their souls. Doesn't that mean they can live?" I asked, hopeful.

"God, you humans are so stupid." He slightly chuckled, "You're remembering what you wish I had said. I said I wouldn't be the one to kill them, honey, but how else could I get their souls?" He looked at me with a smug grin, as if he understood a joke that I didn't.

So someone else will come and kill them, I realized.

I looked around at all the bodies—the smell really started to get around. Not sure where to look, I looked down at my hands, clasping them together, keeping my eyes away from the dead. If I kept looking, I would puke.

"Why did you … " I was unable to finish my sentence, but I was referring to the massacre of everyone here and he could tell. He chuckled, looking around.

"Just having a little fun."

He was truly a monster. "Anyway, I've done so much for you." His face and voice quickly turned harsh, "She's coming for them tonight. It's time for you to pay me back," Alastair said.

She? I thought.

Standing up quickly, Alastair knocked his chair to the ground, reached across the table, and grabbed me by the throat with his bloody hand.

"If you try to warn them again or you try to run, every single person's soul in your family will be mine. I'll kill them all. Every. Single. Member. That includes those cute old people at that home of yours." He then pushed the table away from between us with his other hand, tumbling it to the ground. He lifted me in the air by my throat and hung me in his grip. I was running out of breath, began gurgling, and started to feel lightheaded.

He smiled, dropping me to the ground. I was so dizzy, I fell and landed in a small puddle of blood next to a dead body. He quickly walked away from me and out of the diner. I laid there on the ground in shock.

My phone vibrated in my pocket. Taking it out, I saw that Joshua had texted me.

Chapter 9

I grabbed the gun from Mom's hand and rushed to my room, closing the door quickly behind me and locked it, just in case Mom woke up.

I looked at my phone. Tree had texted back asking about meeting at our tree later, but I just put my phone on the dresser. I couldn't think about that right now. I walked over and sat on my bed with the gun in my hands.

My mom is suicidal? She's all I have, why would she do this to me? I stared at the gun—not even sure where she had even gotten this from. How long had she been considering this? She was never the best mom, but she was the only family I knew. Some tears fell down my cheeks and onto the gun. It sickened me to my stomach that she would have considered leaving me like that.

I mean … maybe she deserves to leave though. I haven't been the best daughter. Life has been so hard on her … my dad left her … so many guys have left her and some clearly abused her. She's messed up … maybe I should do her the favor …

"What the hell? Stop!" I wasn't thinking this. The voice had slipped into my thoughts making me think this—it's never done that before. I usually can differentiate which are my thoughts and which is the voice. It's becoming harder to tell—this scared me.

I got up, took the gun, and laid it on the dresser in front of me. I looked at my reflection in my mirror. I looked so … tired. I had bags under my eyes and I just looked old, too. Older than I should look at this age I think.

Life has been stressful enough, and this voice in my head has lately been getting worse. Now my mom was actually trying to kill herself? I probably should be looking into getting help, for both her *and* me, but we wouldn't be able to afford it, because we'd probably end up needing some real professional help. I would just become more of a burden, too, with all these problems going on in my head. Probably would cost a fortunate to get someone to "fix" me.

I already have been a burden lately anyway, and I've lost my job. I usually helped with the payments for the house as best I could. Now I couldn't.

Things really aren't going to get better, Kate, God said. You might even lose your house … live on the street. Do you want your mother to have to go through that, too?

Tears fell down my cheeks. My world began to warp into something unfamiliar. Nothing changed, everything just felt … unreal. Like as if this was a dream now. I stared at myself in the mirror, my eyes lost their emotion … and my irises looked like they were drained of their color. They looked … gray?

I wasn't looking at myself anymore. I was looking at a girl who looked a lot like me, but couldn't be me. Her eyes looked sad, but angry, too. My heartbeat began speeding up. I started to panic, but my face looked calm and collected in the mirror.

I walked away from the mirror, but at the same time, this wasn't me—it was like I was a prisoner in my own body. This was a nightmare. I really began to panic. I opened my door and walked into the family room, my right hand feeling heavy. This really felt like a dream, I was just awake though—wasn't I? Was this because of the drugs I just took? I only took a couple pills though.

I looked at my mom sleeping on the couch in her drug-induced coma.

Do her the favor, God said.

This must be just a dream, I reasoned with myself, slightly panicked.

Do her the favor!

My right arm seemed to lift itself, feeling heavier than usual. I slowly lifted my hand into my view, realizing the weight in it was the gun. I hadn't realized that I had picked it up when I walked away from my dresser.

Wait. I thought, realization bolting through me like electricity. *This isn't a dream. This is real. I can't do this.*

Do her the favor, God said.

My finger pulled the trigger, shooting my mom right through her head, blood and brains splattering everywhere.

"NO!!!" I shouted, reality washing over me. The world snapped back into place and I was me again, unfortunately.

I dropped the gun in shock. Blood was spread all over the couch and floor. "This … I … what … " I fell to my knees, unsure of how to feel. I felt like crying, but I was still in disbelief.

You killed her, God said, louder and stronger in my head than the voice had ever felt.

It was a man's voice. This couldn't just have been my imagination—this was a *being* talking to me.

Now, you know what you must do next.

"I killed her. What more do you want from me? I killed my own damn mother!" I yelled out loud. Emotions erupted in me and I began to cry uncontrollably. Yes, she wasn't the best mom, but to just end her life like that! I lay on the ground in the fetal position amongst all the blood splattered around the room, crying for what felt like forever.

God didn't say anything. I almost thought the voice was gone until he started talking again over my crying.

Yes, it's what you're here for—to bring death. Now you know what you must do next. Killing your mother was only the beginning.

I stared at the gun lying right in front of me. "No, this stops now," I told God, grabbing the gun and getting up on my knees. I looked at my dead mom for the last time and whispered, "I'm so sorry."

I aimed the gun at my head.

Chapter 10

Your son is dangerous,
He will defy God himself.
The world will burn under his feet and he will smile,
As God dies.

"Earth to Brandon Jones! You've got a call coming in!" yelled a small stocky guy with glasses who was in the next cubicle over.

He knows my name and I don't even remember his right now, Brandon thought to himself. *How have I worked here this long and still can't remember the one guy I sort of talk to at work?*

I snapped out of my day dreaming and looked over at … what's-his-name and said, "Oh, right, thanks … man."

"No problem," he said smiling and then disappeared behind his cubicle wall. *I think his name starts with an S? I wish he would have let me miss this call though.*

Day after day, I have people call me and yell at me about how their TV or their computer, or how both are having problems. I do my best to help them fix it over the phone, but if I have to, I'll send someone to go fix it manually (which is usually what happens).

Yeah, it's just a tech support kind of thing for this tech business. It's a boring job, but I have to help support Jean and my son somehow. I slowly picked up my work phone. I had a cool headset, but I broke it the other day. I had left it on my seat and sat on it by accident, forgetting it was there. So now I was back to using an actual phone, which kind of sucked.

"Hi, my name is Brandon Jones, how can I help you?" I said with a smile into the phone. I know they can't see me but it helps me sound more positive than I actually feel. The yelling then commences.

I hang up my work phone after finally telling the woman on the phone that I was sending someone to fix the TV. It wasn't something I could fix over the phone, but I was still on the phone for about a half hour giving her instructions, but obviously none of them would work. Fixing technology comes so easy to me; I can never fully understand why some people struggle with it so much. I really didn't enjoy this job though. It was times like these that I missed being out on the road with my family.

I feel my cellphone vibrate in my pocket and take it out, seeing a text from Jean. *Hey, Brandon, honey,* even before I keep reading I can tell she needs a favor from me, *Joshua needs a ride home from college, because the van has some problems again.* I was right, *He had gotten a ride from Kate to college but now he needs a ride back and I'm kind of busy here at work. It would help a whole lot if you could maybe go get him?*

That stupid van is getting way too old. *Yeah, no problem,* I write, *I'll probably be able to tell my manager to give me a longer break just to go get Joshua home. Text Joshua for me and let him know I'll be getting him soon. I have to take a few more calls and then I'll head out. Thanks. I love you.* I sent the text as my work phone starts ringing again.

Sam! I finally remember. *That's that guy's name.* I pick up my work phone, "Hi, my name is Brandon, how can I help you?" I say with a smile. The yelling then commences.

Her cellphone vibrates. She wipes some tears away from her cheeks and then looks at the text from Brandon saying he'll get Joshua. I write, "*Thanks, honey, I love you, too. I'll text Joshua.*" and sends the text.

I switch to Joshua's name on my phone and send him a text telling him his dad will get him. After texting Joshua, I turn back towards the small diner and just stare at it, trying to think straight. I had walked outside to the front parking lot to get some air and to get away from all the dead bodies, so I could try to figure out how I'm going to tell the police what happened.

I guess I'll just tell them that some maniac came in and murdered everyone, I thought, while trying to breathe and stay calm. *I wouldn't be lying.* But this wasn't just a murder, it was a massacre. This was so gruesome and insane that I know there will be a ton of questions.

She's coming tonight, I thought to myself, *but who was 'she'? Whoever it is, she's actually going to* ***kill*** *them tonight.* God, I was scared, and frankly felt so stupid.

Back when I made this deal, Alastair made it sound almost harmless. For some reason at the time, I didn't even really think he meant murder when he talked about taking their souls. What an idiot I was—right? I think I've just been in denial, if anything.

I even sort of thought I would have found a way out of this deal by now, too. Ten years is a long time and every day I would think about how I would meet up with this demon and change up the deal, somehow save my son and husband's souls.

Obviously, I never came up with anything. *I have to keep guard tonight. There's no way I can just let this woman walk into my house and take their lives. I have to fight. I have to call the police and report this massacre and then go home right away. Even if that seems suspicious, I'll just tell the police I was scared and ran.*

Taking a deep breath, I regretfully walked back into the diner. I walked around the bodies, ran back to the chefs to tell them what had happened, while calling 911 on my cellphone. When the station answered, I quickly told them over the phone that there had been a murder here in the diner, told them the name of the diner, and hung up. One of the chefs overheard what I said on the phone and ran to the front.

"What happened?" another one of the chefs asked. I ignored him, leaving him with a shocked and confused face, running out the back of the building to where my car was. I heard screams from one of the chefs as the building's door shut behind me. They had seen the massacre.

Chapter 11

Gosh, I've been sitting out here a long time, Joshua Tree thought while sitting outside his community college on a small bench, other people walking in and out of the campus for their classes.

It was hot outside and I would go back inside for the air conditioning, but I hated this education stuff so much that I couldn't get myself to walk back into the building. When I walk out of that building, I'm *done* with it. I don't want to have to walk back in there until my next class on another day.

A girl walked by me with dirty-blonde hair. She was kind of pretty, but didn't really notice me, as she walked towards me. Before she passed, I saw that on her right side, she had dyed her hair green from her roots to her ends in just the front. As she walked away, a breeze blew by and I smelled her pretty fragrance.

Gosh, she's pretty … and smelled good. I watched her as she walked towards the parking lot, not in a creepy way though. I wasn't *watching* her like a weirdo. I was just curious. She got into a white truck and drove away. I sighed to myself. *Totally just got pointlessly distracted … ugh, girls!*

I shouldn't be waiting much longer though, because my mom texted me saying that my dad was going to come get me during his break. Then he texted me about ten minutes ago saying he was on his way, too, so now I wait. I felt a little disappointed, because Kate hasn't responded about meeting me at our tree. I debated with myself whether I'd still go or not. Finally, I see a red car drive up to the college. I get up and start walking towards my dad's car as he drives up.

"Hey, what's up, little tree?" My dad says as I open the door and sit in the car. I throw my backpack into the backseat and the car starts moving as I click my seat belt on and I'm *finally* getting away from school.

"Seriously, dad?" 'Little tree' was the nickname my dad used to call me as a little kid and he still uses it just to bug me now obviously. "I've been too old for that nickname since … well, since I hit puberty, I think."

"Wow, puberty strikes again. Must it take so much away from us parents?" he said jokingly. I decide to stop talking about puberty with my dad and find a way of changing the subject.

"Kind of weird that Mom couldn't come get me; I know she's been working harder lately, but usually her manager or whatever is flexible and stuff."

"Yeah, I'm honestly a little surprised, too." he says, "but I'm sure she's just really busy today." Then he glances over at me with a slight smile, "Your mom told me how you got to school today." I can already tell by his tone what he's getting at.

"Keep your eyes on the road," I said. He chuckled and looked back at the road. "Yes, dad, Kate took me to school today, but that's it—it was just a ride."

"She's a cute girl though," he said, glancing over at me again, as if expecting a response. I really don't know what to say to that, so I just sit here in silence. I don't totally agree with him though—I think she's beautiful.

"Have you tried … "

"Dad, why are you doing this?" I say cutting him off, "We have never talked about this before, so why now?" A part of me wants to talk about this, but at the same time it kind of hurts to talk about. Kate Iris is not as crazy about me as I am for her. I feel it's kind of a losing battle, and to admit that to anyone is just something I don't want to do.

He takes a deep breath and doesn't say anything for at least twenty seconds, which can feel like a very long time. I stare out the window thinking he won't say anything, when he finally says, "I just want you to be happy, little tree."

I turn back towards him, getting ready to call him out on calling me that again, but then I see his face. He looks really sad all of a sudden. He wasn't calling me "little tree" jokingly this time. His eyes stare ahead and they looked … heavy. I realize that he's getting emotional. I haven't seen my dad like this since … well, I can't even remember when I last saw my dad looking like this … don't think I ever have.

"Dad? You OK?" He doesn't answer and just continues talking. He nervously runs his hand through his black, but speckled with white, hair. It's weird, noticing that my dad was aging, I mean.

"I want you to be happy and I want you to live your life to the fullest as much as you can," he said. *Oh boy, this is sounding serious.* "Life is short."

Jesus, this *is* serious. He continued, "Time just flies by and sometimes you make decisions you may regret in the future. Sometimes you miss opportunities that you'll look back on and wish you had taken them. I don't want you to make the wrong decisions, little tree. Important decisions decide what kind of man you're going to be—a good one or a bad one. I just hope you make the good decisions when these times come."

I don't even think he's talking about Kate anymore. I don't

even know how to reply to him after that little speech. He said that as if he knows I will make the wrong decisions. Why would he think that? Does he think I'm a bad person or something? I'm not sure what to say and he seems done talking, too, so we sit in silence for the rest of the ride.

I do want to live life to the fullest. I think to myself, *I want to see her. That's the best decision, I think.*

We finally drove up to the house and my dad pulls into the driveway to drop me off. "All right, Dad, thanks for the ride," I say while getting out of the car, "I'll see you later." I close the passenger door behind me and then open the back seat door, grabbing my backpack.

"No problem, see you later," he replies. I shut the back seat door and start walking up to the house.

Gosh, that was an awkward ride home, I think, as he pulls out of the driveway behind me. I take out my keys, acting like I'm about to open the door. Then, once I hear my dad drive off, I put them back in my pocket and I put my backpack on my grandpa's rocking chair on the porch. I shouldn't be too long and my grandpa's probably taking a nap with my grandma right now.

I quickly walk off towards the cul-de-sac. I walk in between some houses and into the trees behind them going in the direction of the park. The park isn't too far, but it's not that short of a walk, and today is a really hot day in Florida. However, it's worth it to go meet her at our spot under the tree.

Once I finally get to our famous tree meeting spot, I sit down under it. *This tree is amazing.* I think in awe to myself. I realize this almost every time I come to meet Kate here. It's really wide with thick branches and taller than most of the smaller trees around it. There's this empty space from this tree to all the other trees, too. Like as if this is the "mother" tree, watching all the smaller ones grow, keeping an eye on them from a short distance. I look over and touched the little peace sign I carved into the tree.

"*A peace sign?*" Kate had questioned me all those years ago when I first had carved it into the tree. We were probably around fourteen years old. "*Every time I see that, I think of hippies or something,*" she'd say, giggling.

"*Yeah I don't know.*" I had replied. "*I think that it's an important sign, like it's something we all need. Peace. It's how the world really should be—peaceful.*" She looked at me smiling for a few moments. I probably sounded ridiculous to her.

"*Well, Tree, I think you found your calling. You're going to have to try and find some way to unite the world in peace ... good luck with that.*" she said jokingly with that beautiful smile of hers.

Remembering that brought a small smile to my face. I took my hand off the peace sign. I hope Kate doesn't take too long—it really is hot and I'm already feeling a bit sweaty from the walk. I sit listening to some birds, a dog barking in the distance, and then a squirrel crawling down the tree near me. It makes a weird noise that I haven't ever really heard a squirrel make before. It's kind of funny and I laugh to myself. The squirrel gets down from the tree and gets a bit closer to me than I would like. *This squirrel must not be that scared of humans,* I think. I take my attention off the squirrel and look at my phone.

I text Kate that I'm here, but she doesn't text back, so I just sit here waiting some more. I look up from my phone and realize that the squirrel is gone, which makes me feel lonely all of a sudden.

Things really haven't felt right between us lately. Not between the squirrel and me—between Kate and me. I mean, I understand she may need her space, but why can't she enjoy my company as much as she used to? Or at least, as much as I *thought* she did?

Why does she seem not to enjoy my company as much as I enjoy hers? Even if she doesn't have the same feelings that I do, wouldn't she still at least enjoy being my friend? It's always good to have someone just to share your thoughts and feelings. It sucks to feel like I may not be that person for her anymore, when she definitely is that person for me. Well, used to be now.

Lately it's been getting on my nerves the way she obviously ignores me, so I just want to ignore her back, but that's easier said than done. We may just be drifting as we get older, which really sucks. But I guess that's what happens as you get older—people take their different paths.

Damn it, why won't she text me back. I'm having these stupid thoughts again. I need some kind of distraction. I stand up and just wander a little farther from the tree. I look between the smaller trees that separate the park from our meeting spot. It's almost completely empty in the park.

I finally sigh. *She's not going to come obviously,* I regretfully accept. I turn off my cellphone, more out of frustration if anything—I don't want to keep looking at it.

I walk back to our tree and just put my hand on it, closing my eyes and taking a deep breath. I hear thunder in the distance—it's going to rain. I open my eyes and regretfully take my hand off the tree, turning around to start walking back to my house.

What a disappointing day.

Chapter 12

I probably just creeped Joshua out with that little talk, Brandon Tree thought as he drove back home from work. He hadn't really thought about how he actually made Joshua feel during the little speech he gave while driving him home until now.

I either creeped him out or made him uncomfortable at the very least. It had to be said though, I thought to myself. It did have to be said. Back when I had lung cancer, I had an extremely realistic dream. In it, this man with glowing white irises and white hair visited me; he also wore a white cape, which was kind of weird, too. It sounds insane and I would have not let it affect me as much as it has, but the message he gave me still brings chills down my spine. The words continue to echo in my head almost every day since. First he told me he was an angel of God and then he said,

Your son is dangerous, this so called "angel" had said to me.

He will defy God himself.
The world will burn under his feet
and he will smile as God dies

It seemed crazy and I didn't want to believe my son would be "dangerous." The way this angel described him did seem incredibly over-exaggerated, but those words have echoed in my head all these years. I had at least to make sure Joshua grew up to be a good man, like any dad should at least. *So it had to be said,* I thought, convincing myself.

I drove up to our house and parked in our driveway behind Jean's small black car. I got out of my car and felt a small drop of water on my arm, then heard a bit of thunder in the distance.

Gonna rain. I thought. I started walking down the driveway, passing by the van. *Well, I have to find some way of fixing this piece of junk. Little tree needs some kind of transportation.* I continue on my way to the front door when it flew open. Jean stood there with her eyes wide open in fear.

"Where's Joshua?" she asked with a shaky voice, holding his backpack.

It starts raining as he walks back to his neighborhood through a small forest that separated the park from his neighborhood.

You'd think that the rain would make me at least walk faster, but honestly, I just feel like walking in the rain right now. I'll get home soaked, but I could care less in this moment. I continue to walk, when this chill runs down my spine. This feeling is so intense I actually stop walking.

I look around and see nothing but trees. *What's wrong with me?* I think to myself, *there's nobody around.* I keep walking forward when I hear a twig break behind me. I quickly turn and see a man with white hair, white clothes, and strangely … a white cape. Yeah, he really looked weird. I kind of squeal in surprise.

He was standing behind me a few yards away. His skin looked so pale—inhumanly pale. His eyes are really what kept me from moving though. The irises were a mix of mostly white and some gray. He almost looked like a blind person, but he was looking at me like he could see me, so I'm pretty sure he wasn't.

His eyes actually looked kind of beautiful, so I can't help but stare. I almost got the urge to walk towards him while he just stood there, staring at me with his strange eyes. I was so distracted by how pretty his eyes were that it took me a bit to realize that he looked angry. I finally come to my senses, turn around, and quickly walk away, forcing myself not to glance behind me, still feeling his strange eyes burning a hole in the back of my head.

I walk out of the forest and between two houses, my shoes finally meeting the wet road. I walk through the middle of the cul-de-sac and towards my house.

That man didn't look like the guy from my nightmare. The guy in my nightmare, the man with the beard, actually looked like the one who had shot my dad in Ohio all those years ago. *But his eyes … those were familiar,* I thought.

The guy in Ohio literally had black irises. *Wait no … they had changed color, too.* I slowly started to recall my nightmare. Sounds strange, but his eyes were what haunted me still to this day. In my recent nightmare, his eyes would slowly just change from black to white, too. That's what was so familiar about the guy in the forest.

Chills ran down my spine. *I really need someone to talk to; I might be losing my mind. I guess it can't be Kate though—she needs this space,* I think to myself, frustrated. I really just missed her.

When I finally reach my house, I see that both my parents' cars are parked in the driveway and my backpack isn't on the rocking chair where I had left it.

"Crap," I whisper to myself. I walk up to my house and I hear someone screaming inside the house over the pitter-patter of the rain. I'm pretty sure it's my mom. As I get closer, I'm positive that it is her.

"I swear to GOD, I'm going to call the POLICE if he doesn't answer his cellphone!" my mom screams, probably at my grandparents or Dad. *Oh crap, my cellphone.* I had forgotten to turn it back on. But why is my mom freaking out so much? She isn't normally like this. She actually is pretty damn carefree and rarely ever gets angry. Both my parents are like that actually—what's different about today?

I notice the door is still slightly open so I slowly bring my wet hand up to the doorknob to push it open. Before I can even push the door, it swings open and my mom is standing there with a phone up to her ear, her eyes go wide.

"Joshua!! Oh, thank God," she says as she wraps her arms around me. "You're soaked! Where have you been?" On the phone, I hear a small voice answer, "*911 what's your emergency?*" but my mom hangs up right away.

Man, she was serious about calling the cops, I think to myself, surprised and confused, *something must be wrong.*

"Um … well I just went for a walk in the park, Mom. I just needed some air and I didn't realize it would rain … or that you would be freaking out so much. Are you OK?" I asked her as she pulls me into the house and closes the door, aggressively locking it.

"A guy came into the diner today. He killed almost everyone in it." she said, almost a bit too simply, as if this was old news.

"What! Are you OK? Did he try and hurt you? How did you … "

"I'm fine. You shouldn't have been out just walking around with a murderer on the loose," she said cutting me off and started walking away.

"Well, I didn't know, Mom." I said slightly annoyed. She didn't even acknowledge my questions and just went back towards the kitchen. "He's here, he's fine." she said.

"I told you," I heard my dad say.

After taking a shower and drying off, I changed into my gym shorts and a white shirt to get more comfortable, ate some dinner and then went to my room. I regretfully worked on a small assignment for one of my classes on my laptop and then got ready for bed.

I opened my door. "Goodnight, guys," I called out to anyone in general.

"Goodnight," I heard my mom and grandma call out. My dad and grandpa were probably either watching TV or already asleep in their rooms.

My grandma would probably have been in her room with my grandpa already, but she was keeping an eye on my mom, who was still acting strange. She didn't seem to want to go to bed and just sat on the couch, staring at the TV, which had the news on. From what I could sort of hear from my room, I could tell they were still talking about the "massacre at a small diner" on the news. I closed my door behind me and lay in bed.

It was also on some major news channels, since it was such a crazy story. A lot of people died and I'm afraid it scarred my mom or something—like mentally. She wouldn't really talk about it and anytime any of us would try and push her to talk about it, she would just ignore us.

It really scared me though, the fact that they didn't catch this person—or people. It couldn't have been one person; so many people had been murdered. What also was strange was how my mom was completely unharmed. I was thankful that she wasn't hurt, but what I saw from the news was that basically everyone in that diner was killed. How did she get away?

I lay in my bed wide-awake just thinking about all of this. It wasn't just this news that kept me up though. It took a while for me to fall asleep anyway, because the nightmares have been getting worse. The only way I could get myself to sleep was to lay here until I was exhausted and my body had no choice. That normally took hours, but slowly I started to drift.

He stared at me with those evil black eyes, his black irises glowing.

Blood dripped off his face and beard … he smiled.

The man with the white eyes, white hair, and white cape stood not far behind him. He stared angrily at me.

The black-eyed man slowly walked towards me with that ugly grin. "It's time," he said, but it sounded muffled. He continued to walk towards me and then stopped a couple of inches away.

"It's time," he repeated, still sounding muffled.

I realized there was glass separating him from me.

He lifted his bloody hand—in it was a gun.

He tapped on the glass with it. *tap tap* *tap tap*

TAP TAP

TAP TAP I woke up and jumped off my bed right onto my feet. Someone was actually tapping on my window outside. Was it the murderer? Was it that strange man in the forest? Was he the murderer? I was about to yell, but then I heard her voice.

"Tree, are you in there?"

Kate? I opened my blinds—it was actually her. She kneeled

outside and had a gun in her hand, which she was using it to tap on the window.

"Kate, what the hell are you doing here?" I asked her through the glass. Even if it was her, I still felt cautious about opening the window, especially since she had a gun with her. Why did she have a gun?

"It's OK, I promise, let me in. I just need to talk." she said. I hesitated. I looked at her face—she did look desperate. Her eyes looked … different though. It was too dark to tell outside, but I could still see something different about them. "All right, fine" I said, unlocking my window and opening it.

She crawled through my window and into my room. She was wearing tight black pants and a black shirt. It wasn't raining as hard as it was earlier, but it was still drizzling, so she was kind of wet and she was barefoot, which was odd. She moved past me and I got a whiff of her. It wasn't perfume … more of her natural Kate Iris smell, which I loved of course.

Oh boy … she smelled nice. *Oh jeez … don't lose your cool.* While I smelled her … amazingness, another aroma slowly made its way to me, which wasn't as pleasant. I couldn't really see, so it was hard to tell what it was. It smelled … metallic-like though.

This is really weird and probably shouldn't be happening, I thought, feeling uncomfortable. Kate has been in my room before, but never at this time. What time was it anyways? This question and a couple of others flowed out of me.

"What time is it? Why are you here this late? Why are you barefoot? And why the hell do you have a gun, Kate?" I asked whispering, as I closed my window and turned to find her sitting on my floor.

"I don't know. I had to get out of my house. I couldn't be there any longer … " She said sounding and looking tired. I walked to my door and locked it—just in case. Then I walked over to Kate and sat in front of her. It was still dark, but I could see that her cheeks were red—she had been crying.

Without even thinking about it, I lifted my hand and touched her cheek. *Her eyes are gray,* I thought to myself as I looked at them and she looked at me. That was odd, because her eyes weren't normally that color and I don't think they change either. *They look familiar ... almost like the man in the forest.* I put my hand down when I realized that I was being weird. I felt embarrassed.

"Kate ... your eyes."

"My mom's dead," she barely whispered. My stomach felt like it dropped.

"Oh my God ... how ... was it the murderers on the news? Was she at the diner?" It was the first thing I could think of.

"No," she said. I could tell she was on the brink of crying again. Then, almost feeling dumb about how long it took me to notice, I saw blood stains on her shirt and pants. *That's what I had smelled,* I realized. "Kate?" I hesitated—I didn't really want to ask.

"I killed her," she said.

Chapter 13

Jean woke up suddenly in the middle of the night and sat up as fast as she could, realizing that she had fallen asleep on the couch. The TV was still on and was the only light in the room. Jean looked around, feeling a weird panic in her gut. She turned the TV off, shrouding the room in total darkness.

Brandon, Joshua, and my dad had probably all gone to bed already. My mom was lying on the recliner chair near the couch and had fallen asleep in it, too. She couldn't convince me to go to bed, so she stayed up to keep an eye on me. I could tell my family was worried about me, but I couldn't risk telling them about the situation or I would risk losing everyone—not just Brandon and Joshua.

I had to stay up all night, just in case Alastair—or whoever he was sending—was coming tonight, but I guess I had accidently fallen asleep. I got up off the couch and decided to get a bat from the closet in the living room—might as well have a weapon.

I took a few steps from the couch when I realized I heard voices. I heard Joshua's voice scream something. A gunshot sounded from somewhere in the house. My stomach flipped and I felt like I was going to throw up.

"NO!!" I screamed and began running. I sprinted towards Joshua's room—I had to protect my son. I tried to open the door, but it was locked. "Joshua!" I yelled, but I didn't even bother to wait on a reply. I backed up, ran forward, and kicked the door, putting all my weight into it.

Somehow I smashed it open on the first kick, which was surprising. When I looked in, I saw Joshua standing there with a gun in his hand and Kate Iris lying on the ground face up, dead with a bullet hole in her head, the room covered in blood. Blood flowed around her head, like a halo.

5 Minutes Ago

You idiot girl, God said in Kate's head.

He sounded angry. Angrier than I have ever heard him, admitting this to Tree was not what he seemed to want.

"You what? You killed your own mother?" Tree stood up in shock and backed up away from me.

"Tree, you have to believe me!" I pleaded. "Yes, I did, but it wasn't me! God made me do it!" I admitted. *Shit*, I thought, *just said the "G" word. I'm sure that sounds insane.*

He stood there looking at me, and then looked away. I could tell he was conflicted. I couldn't blame him—I would be, too. "Ugh! That sounds crazy, but I promise it's the truth!" I said standing up. *Now is the time to come clean.*

He won't believe you, you stupid girl.

"Were you … the one who killed those people at the diner?" He quickly asked before I could say anything else. He looked like he was going to be sick.

"The one your mom works at? What exactly happened at the diner?" I asked. "I haven't watched the news or anything." He had just mentioned the murderer at the diner when we were sitting down, but honestly, I was so nervous about telling him I murdered my mom I didn't completely think about what he said.

He didn't answer though—he just stared at me.

He thinks you're a murderer. He thinks you're evil.

I had to say anything I could to fix this. Tree has always been there for me and I can't lose him, too. I never really had a family, even when my mom was alive. She didn't care about me much. Tree was as close as family as I felt I had—if I lost him, too …

"No, Tree, listen, I haven't killed anyone else. But something has changed, like, inside of me."

Maybe you are evil, God said.

I tried to ignore it. "Tree, there's been this voice inside of me telling me to hate you and … kill you."

Because you should.

"But I've been fighting it all this time"

You can't trust him.

"And it's been telling me to kill … other people, too."

All of them deserved to die.

"But I haven't, I promise,"

You should have.

"And today it took me over and made me kill my mom!"

Because you're weak and she deserved it!

I grabbed my head, struggling even to get my words out over His voice. "Shut up!" I yelled at the voice. "God made me kill my mom and I was going to kill myself afterwards, but I couldn't make myself to do it! God wouldn't let me, because he has some kind of hold on me and I can still feel it on me right now!"

Tree stared at me in shock. I wanted him to say something so bad, but what could he say? I realized that maybe this was unfixable.

Something inside me broke.

Look at his stupid face. So stupid. I never loved him. Love?

He'll never understand. I never liked him. Did he love me?

He hates me. But I love him. It's the only way out.

I hate him. No! Why would I love him? I have to stop this.

He doesn't care. He never cared. Maybe he does care?

NO. I should kill him. Love is weakness. Love is a lie. He doesn't love me. Why would he love me? No. I don't care. Death. Chaos. This has to end. Kill him. They all should die. This has to end. I'll kill myself Kill.

Just do it. I don't want to die. Why?

Get out of my head! Please stop. He doesn't care.

WHO ARE YOU? Kill him not yourself.

I can't. You can. I can't

I never cared about him either.

This has to end.

That's it. I give up.

I lifted the gun to my head, aiming it at my temple.

"Kate, whoa, no! Wait!" Tree yelled, darting for the gun, but it was too late. I pulled the trigger and everything went dark.

I'm dead. *I am dead right?*

I felt a presence.

God??

The voice chuckled. *I am your father, Kate.*

But no, I'm not God. Don't worry.

Your part in this story isn't over yet.

Not even close.

My name is Nicholas.

Chapter 14

"Kate, whoa, no! Wait!" I yelled as I saw her put the gun up to her head.

I darted forward to grab the gun but I was too late. She shot herself in the head, blood and … probably brains flew out of her head. She let go of the gun as she dropped and I got my hand around it. She fell onto her back on the floor with a *thud.* I now had the gun in my hand and backed away in shock.

What the hell just happened? I stood there in shock with the gun in my hand. She was dead. Kate just committed suicide right in front of me. I couldn't stop her, and I was right here.

I heard my mom at my door trying to open it. "Joshua!" she yelled. I couldn't get myself to say anything or yell back. It didn't matter though, because she came smashing in. She actually broke my door open. She stared at me. I ripped my eyes off Kate's dead body and looked my mom in the eyes. I realized what it probably looked like.

"Mom, I didn't … she shot herself! I couldn't stop her in time!" I fell to my knees in front of Kate's dead body, dropping the gun next to me. She lay on her back, staring blankly up at the ceiling.

Blood dripped from her head, causing a halo of blood to pool around her. *She really is gone,* I thought as I looked at her blank stare. My mind couldn't even wrap around the fact I would never see her laugh, or cry, or smile again. I couldn't keep myself together.

I began to cry uncontrollably.

I watched as my son sobbed over Kate's dead body. I stared as he cried over the corpse of his best friend.

My whole leg throbbed from kicking the door in. Hopefully, I didn't break anything, but my mind was in shock, so I ignored the pain.

This is not how tonight was supposed to go, I thought. I mean, I was glad my son was alive, but something still didn't feel right. Kate didn't even try to kill Joshua, it seemed. It couldn't have been this simple.

"What's going on? Did I hear a gun shot? Did you break open the door?" I heard Brandon call as he ran over, with my mom closely behind him. "How did you … oh my God." He whispered as he saw the scene. My mom screamed when she came around from behind him and saw it, too. She quickly turned to walk away, just as my dad was walking down the hallway, too.

"Don't go over there. You don't want to see," my mom said, grabbing him and taking him to the kitchen, where I heard her begin to puke. I looked at Brandon.

"Can you make sure Mom's OK?" I asked him. He slowly nodded, looking at Joshua crying over Kate.

"Yeah, I'll go grab a mop. I'll go get the phone, too, and call the police," Brandon said, looking like he was going to be sick himself, but I could tell he tried to act strong for me.

"You can bring the phone to me, honey, I'll make the call." I said, knowing he didn't want to talk. He looked at me and nodded gratefully. Then he made his way towards the kitchen where my mom and dad were.

I stared at Kate's dead body. Then I noticed something that made my stomach drop. Her eyes blinked.

Chapter 15

"Joshua!" my mom yelled at me. Before I even had time to react, Kate sat up and grabbed me by the throat.

She squeezed my throat with amazing strength, so I struggled to get even a small breath. She stared at me for a second, with those new ghostly gray eyes, and I stared back in disbelief. Blood still dripped out of the hole on the side of her head where she shot herself. The hole stopped bleeding and healed instantly and so did the huge hole on the other side of her head. I almost thought she was going to just let go, but then she threw me into the air, right into the wall above my bed and I fell down onto it. I gasped for air and started to get up slowly, because I was feeling a bit lightheaded.

Kate, now on her feet, leaned down to grab the gun, but my mom tackled her to the ground.

"Mom wait! She's really … " before I could even finish the sentence Kate pushed my mom off her, so she went flying into the ceiling and came crashing down onto the ground … "strong."

She didn't get up from the ground—I hoped she was just knocked out, but before I could think much more about it, Kate floated (yes, floated!) back onto her feet. She then leaned down and grabbed the gun off the ground.

My dad ran into the room with a mop. "What's going on

now? Jean!" he yelled noticing Mom on the ground, and then he looked away from her and at Kate, dropping the mop in shock. "Kate?" She looked at him with an ice-cold stare.

This moment seemed to go in slow motion for me. I'm not really sure why it did, but my brain just couldn't comprehend that this would ever actually happen.

First, I looked at Kate and saw the strangest thing. Her irises went from gray, to black. That almost made me sick—they were the same color as the killer's eyes years ago—the one that haunted me in my nightmares. She then lifted her arm, aimed the gun at my dad, and shot him. The bullet hit him directly in the middle of his head and his body crumpled to the ground right next to the mop.

"DAD!!!" I yelled, time seeming to go back to normal. I got off my bed, but stopped moving when I saw the blood pooling around him. I felt sick.

"One," Kate said, as if killing my dad was just on her checklist. She then turned the gun on me. Her irises then turned gray again, "Two."

Finally, rid the world of this monster. Nicholas said in Kate's head as she aimed the gun at Joshua Tree. This had to be done.

I got ready to pull the trigger and fire this bullet into his head.

Wait! Another voice said in my head, which took me by surprise. I didn't pull the trigger. Joshua stood in front of me, looking scared and confused.

"Kate?" he said questioningly. He had so much emotion behind the way he said my name, but I couldn't understand those emotions anymore—I wasn't Kate Iris anymore.

Wait? Wait for what!! He's right here! We kill him and we're done!! His father is dead, so you can have his soul. Now let me have Joshua's soul!

Nicholas yelled in my head, clearly angry and frustrated. Who was he talking to?

The other voice entered my head again. This presence felt so different from Nicholas. It felt darker. I felt it take me over a few seconds ago when I killed Tree's dad, but it hadn't talked until now.

Yes, wait, it said. How did you bring this girl, Kate, back to life? When did you get that powerful? There was no reply. Nicholas obviously didn't want to answer that.

Don't want to reveal your new tricks, huh? OK, well, also, rid the world of him? How important is Joshua Tree's soul? Maybe we changed our mind on the agreement, the dark presence said. I felt Nicholas grow angrier.

WE?? You mean the soul was for … Nicholas was about to explode with anger.

Yes. And we want both of these souls, the dark presence said with what felt like a forced kind of calmness.

NO, I am not having this! Nicholas screamed in my head so loudly it caused me to flinch.

Tree grabbed the gun from my hand while I was distracted by the voices. He aimed the gun at me. "Kate, I don't want to do this," he said with a shaky voice. "Tree, run!" the old Kate would have yelled at him, but she didn't exist anymore. She died when she shot herself in the head.

That's it, Nicholas said, taking full control of my body.

I raised my hand towards Joshua Tree and felt this unexplainable power. My body felt stronger than ever. I looked at Joshua Tree. He looked like nothing but an ant that had to be squished. I saw the fear in his eyes and I enjoyed it.

I lifted my hand and he went flying as if hit by an invisible force. The gun flew out of his hand and fell next to my foot, he slammed into the wall above his bed and I held him there against it. He hung against the wall, as if held up by nothing, and screamed in pain. I was actually holding him up by his soul. I felt it almost like it was actually in my hand.

"Finally," Nicholas said using my mouth, my voice, my body. He completely controlled me now. I could feel Joshua Tree's soul pulsing in my hand. He screamed in pain. It must be painful to have someone hold your soul. Well, this will get even more painful, Nicholas said in my head.

I began slowly to close my hand, crushing his soul, slowly killing Joshua Tree.

Chapter 16

"Kate Iris! Wake up, Kate Iris!" Kate slowly woke up and lifted her head off her desk, hearing the other kids in class snickering.

Nine Years Ago

I regretfully look up to see my fourth grade teacher looking flustered. "It may be the last day, but you still can't just sleep through class Ms. Iris," she said with her hands on her hips—being a bit overdramatic if you ask me.

"Sorry, Mrs. Perry," I say, feeling really embarrassed that she had to call me out in front of the whole class. Luckily, the day was almost over. For the rest of class, Mrs. Perry just talked about how this was a great year and how she hopes that we have a great year of fifth grade next year. How she thinks we're prepared, but shouldn't stop preparing and blah blah blah.

I didn't really enjoy this year of fourth grade and I'm not that excited about going to fifth. I barely knew anyone, because I was one of those new kids who just walked in during the middle of the year. I used to live in New York with my mom and stepfather, but they got a divorce and my mom couldn't afford living in New York anymore. So here I am now, living in Florida, and I haven't really made many friends, because I'm not much of a talker. I kind of hate other people actually.

The bell finally rings, meaning it's the end of the day, and a year of fourth grade. I sigh with a sense of relief and grab my backpack off the back of my chair, as Mrs. Perry takes us outside toward the bus loop. Once we're at the bus loop, I look around for the one friend I actually had made when I got here, Lizzy. She wasn't in my class unfortunately.

I actually met her on my first day of school. It was the end of my first day of school and I was on my way home on the bus. I was really tired from the long day and started to drift and fall asleep, but then I sensed someone sitting next to me, so I woke up kind of startled. She was a skinny girl, and we actually looked kind of similar, I thought, except her hair was a bit lighter.

She had dirty blonde hair, but what I found really cool was that she also had strands of hair dyed green on the front-right side of her head. The dyed green hair started at the top and went all the way down to her ends. It was so cool, because I never seen anyone my age with dyed hair before. Another cool thing about her was her eyes. They were a bright green, which kind of matched her hair. I never saw anything like them—mine were so boring compared to hers. They were strange, seemed almost to glow slightly—so pretty.

"*Hi, I'm Lizzy,*" she had said. "*You're really pretty.*" I remember her saying, and I remember me just being really awkward at first by replying, "*uh ... thanks. Your hair ... and eyes ... are nice.*" That made her giggle, but it was kind of an awkward ride home that day. But she continued to sit next to me on the bus and, of course, over time we became best friends.

So now, I was searching for her at the bus loop on the last day of school. I finally spotted her sitting on a bench away from everyone. I guess she never made any other friends either. We didn't have class together, so I wasn't really sure how she was around other kids. I never minded it just being us though.

"Hey, Lizzy," I said with a smile as I walked over and sat next to her. She turned to me, revealing her cool green-dyed hair on her right side, and smiled back at me, looking at me with those pretty green eyes. I was so jealous of her look. "Hey, Kate, it's the last day. Crazy right? Went really fast," she said.

"Definitely, but I'm so glad it is. I hope this summer lasts forever!" I said. Lizzy laughed a little, thinking I was joking. "I'm not joking," I said even though I was laughing a little too, but that was just because she laughed. "I really just don't find school fun." She looked at me, still slightly giggling.

"What?" I asked her.

"I feel like you don't find anything fun. You have to not be so serious all the time, Kate." Lizzy said. She was right; I had to learn to lighten up. It just felt hard sometimes. I felt lonely a lot, and I didn't exactly know how *not* to feel this way. I was lonely, but most people I knew seemed always to hurt me, so I put walls up. I was even like this back in New York—I never had a friend like Lizzy. We talked a lot and got along, it was kind of weird.

I saw my teacher walking over to where I sat. *Oh gosh, what does she want?* I thought. She stopped right in front of me and looked a little confused, saying, "How come you're over here alone?" Now I looked at her confused.

"I'm not, I'm here with … " I looked to my side and Lizzy was gone. "She was just here a second ago." How did she walk away so fast? Then I looked over and saw her getting on our bus. "Oh, our bus is here!" I said standing up.

How did Lizzy move so fast? And why didn't she tell me our bus was here? "Have to go, Mrs. Perry. Bye," I said while quickly walking away.

"OK, have a good summer, Kate," she called after me, still

looking a bit concerned. I didn't know why, but I didn't care. I probably wouldn't ever see her again as my teacher, so I just ran over to my bus. I walked onto the bus and found Lizzy in our seat looking out the window at the kids out on the bus loop. I sat down next to her. "How did you … "

"Hey, you want to hang out at the park tomorrow?" she said turning towards me. I was taken aback, since she just cut me off, but became excited, because she wanted to hang out.

"Oh yeah, totally!" I said excited, probably a bit too excited though. The bus started moving once everyone was on it, as Lizzy and I just talked and planned on when and where we were going to meet at the park the next day.

"There's this amazing tree that I want to show you. You have to go through a small forest, but you'll find it. It's a great meeting spot," she said, looking excited.

I nodded and said, "OK, I know my mom won't mind me walking to the park." She wouldn't mind, because she wouldn't know. She's always too busy with her new boyfriend and stuff. "But will your parents be OK with that?"

"Oh, yeah, no problem, they don't mind. The park isn't far from where I live," she said.

We talked a little more about our plans to meet at the park and she gave me directions to the tree where we were going to meet. Then we talked a bit more about our plans for summer in general and once the bus paused at Lizzy's stop, she stood up. I got up and moved into the walkway, so she could get by.

A kid with black hair behind me groaned when I got in his way on the bus aisle. It was David—I knew his name, because he was this annoying boy in my class.

"What are you doing?" he said aggravated. "I'm letting my friend get off at her stop." I said annoyed. Everything I did just seemed to get on people's nerves always and I didn't know why.

"Friend?" David said confused. Lizzy quickly walked in front of me and down the aisle, not even saying bye. I was about to call out bye to her when David pushed me back into my seat. "You're such a weirdo," he said, walking down the aisle and out of the bus.

Why was he so confused about us being friends? Is it really that shocking that I would have a friend? I sat there angrily as the bus pulled away. As the bus drove from the stop, I saw Lizzy turn back towards the bus, waving bye to me. I waved back.

A kid with curly long red hair and glasses popped up from the seat in front of me. "Why do you talk to yourself?" he asked.

I looked at him confused. "What? Who are you?" I asked him.

"I'm Billy." he said as if I should have already known his name. "Why do you talk to yourself?" Billy asked. "I've been sitting in front of you for a while and you've been talking to yourself for the whole year. Do you have an imaginary friend?"

Are you freaking kidding me? I thought getting more annoyed. "I've been talking to my friend, Lizzy. Clearly you need to get your glasses checked. Probably should get your ears checked too while you're at it. Now leave me alone, *Billy*" I said starting to get angry.

He realized I was starting to get mad, so he turned around in his seat where I couldn't see him again. This kid, Billy, was obviously making fun of Lizzy, acting like she didn't exist or something. *Gosh people can be so annoying,* I thought. The bus finally reached my stop and I eagerly got off.

Once I finally got home, I heard my mom with her boyfriend in her room. I didn't know what they were doing, but I just heard a lot of groaning and moaning. So ... gross stuff I'm thinking.

I went to the kitchen and made myself my own dinner, which

was just a sad sandwich. I was used to making my own dinner, since my mom was always on drugs, working, or with some new boyfriend. I grabbed a cup from the sink and poured myself a cup of water.

I took my sandwich and my cup of water to the living room, sat on the couch, and watched TV for the rest of the day. My mom came out once and just said a quick ,"Hi," grabbed some food from the kitchen and went back to her room with her boyfriend. More moaning came out of the room.

A few hours later, after watching some mind-numbing television, it started to get late and I felt tired, so I turned off the TV, walked to the kitchen, cleaned my plate and cup, and went to my room. I dressed in my pajamas and got into bed to get ready to *try* to sleep. Yes, TRY to sleep.

As if right on schedule, the yelling began between my mom and her new boyfriend. What they fought about I never knew and could care less. But it always would start late at night and last for hours.

They would yell at each other and I would just lay here, unable to sleep for most of the night, because of the loud yelling. But this night was slightly different, because I lay in my bed excited for tomorrow. I couldn't wait to meet Lizzy at the park and just hang out. It's been so long since I hung out with a friend.

I think I have made my first real best friend, I thought, smiling to myself. Eventually I was able to drift into sleep over the yelling and shouting outside my door.

Chapter 17

The next morning I woke up excited and got ready to meet Lizzy at the park. I dressed, combed my hair, brushed my teeth, and walked to the kitchen to make myself an egg to eat. Once I was done eating, I just walked outside and started off towards the park. That's how easy it was to avoid my mom, who was either out doing who knows what or sleeping in her room. Today I was thankful about it, so that I could set off for the park without any problems.

I quickly walked for about fifteen minutes or so and finally reached the park. I followed the directions that Lizzy told me and walked to the middle of the park, which was a clearing with nothing but grass and a couple of trees. I turned until the playground was on my left and the parking lot was in front of me like she told me. I looked to my right and saw the small forest that I should walk through. I started off towards it.

I hiked through trees, sticks, and leaves crunching and cracking under my feet. I was walking for about a minute until I came upon the small clearing and saw the tree Lizzy had told me about. It actually took my breath away.

It was amazing how different it felt compared to all of the other trees around it. It was so much thicker, wider, and taller than the others. Its branches were thick enough for a tree house to be set somewhere in there and its leaves were all green, but looked like different shades of green. There was a short clearing from the other smaller trees all around it. It was amazing, and it actually made me feel like as if I were in the middle of the world.

I didn't see Lizzy anywhere as I looked around. *Weird,* I thought, *she told me that she would most likely be waiting for me.* I tried not to think much about it. *She's probably on her way.* I walked up to the tree and sat down by it. This was the first time I had gone to this park. It was nice I guess, but I hated bugs.

I didn't have any way of keeping track of time, but it started to feel like it had been awhile. As I sat back on the tree, a small squirrel made its way down the tree nearby me. It probably came a little closer than I would have liked, but it was kind of cute. It made a funny noise, which made me giggle, and then ran off. I smiled.

Well, that was just kind of weird. I looked around and had a small sinking feeling when I realized that maybe she wasn't going to show up.

But she seemed excited about it! Why would she invite me and then not come? I felt tears slowly coming to my eyes. *No,* I thought to myself and stopped crying. *I can't let someone else make me cry over them. Just forget her.*

I wiped away a tear that had escaped my eye and stood up. I was about to walk away, when I heard some sticks and leaves cracking—it sounded like steps. Someone was walking around from the other side of the tree. "Lizzy?" I called out, thinking it was her. The crunching of the feet got closer and I saw a boy walk from the other side of the tree.

He looked a bit shocked to see me there and stopped. "Oh … hi. No, I'm not Lizzy." He looked away from me and just stood there awkwardly, and so did I. We really didn't know what to say to each other. He was kind of cute, with his short brown, slightly curly hair. He started to turn to walk away, when I decided to push myself.

"Wait," I said with a slightly shaky voice. He stopped and looked back. "I'm Kate Iris. Uh, what's your name?"

"Oh, well, my name is Joshua … Tree," he said. Something about that name changed something in me. I can't really explain it exactly, but it felt like something woke up inside me. I think that's the best way I can explain it. It didn't feel good though, but I ignored it. This kid seemed nice, but I had just met him. There was no reason not to like him.

"Tree? Your last name is Tree?" I asked. He nodded, and I could tell that something about telling me that seemed to be embarrassing for him. It was kind of funny and I started to giggle slightly. When he looked more embarrassed, I thought, *Oh jeez, don't make him feel bad.*

"Well, actually, I think that's pretty cool!" I said. He looked at me a bit confused, but I could tell that made him feel a little better. "It would make sense if our hangout is under this tree. Right, *Mr. Tree?*"

"Hangout?" he asked, looking confused. I looked around thinking about Lizzy. I looked back at Joshua Tree and decided she didn't matter—maybe I didn't need her.

"Yeah, this could be our spot—come sit. How old are you, Tree?" I asked while he walked over and sat down. I sat next to him. "I'm ten," he said while looking at me. He had nice brown eyes.

"Oh, me, too," I replied. That's when I heard a voice that would change my life forever. It whispered in my head.

Hate him.

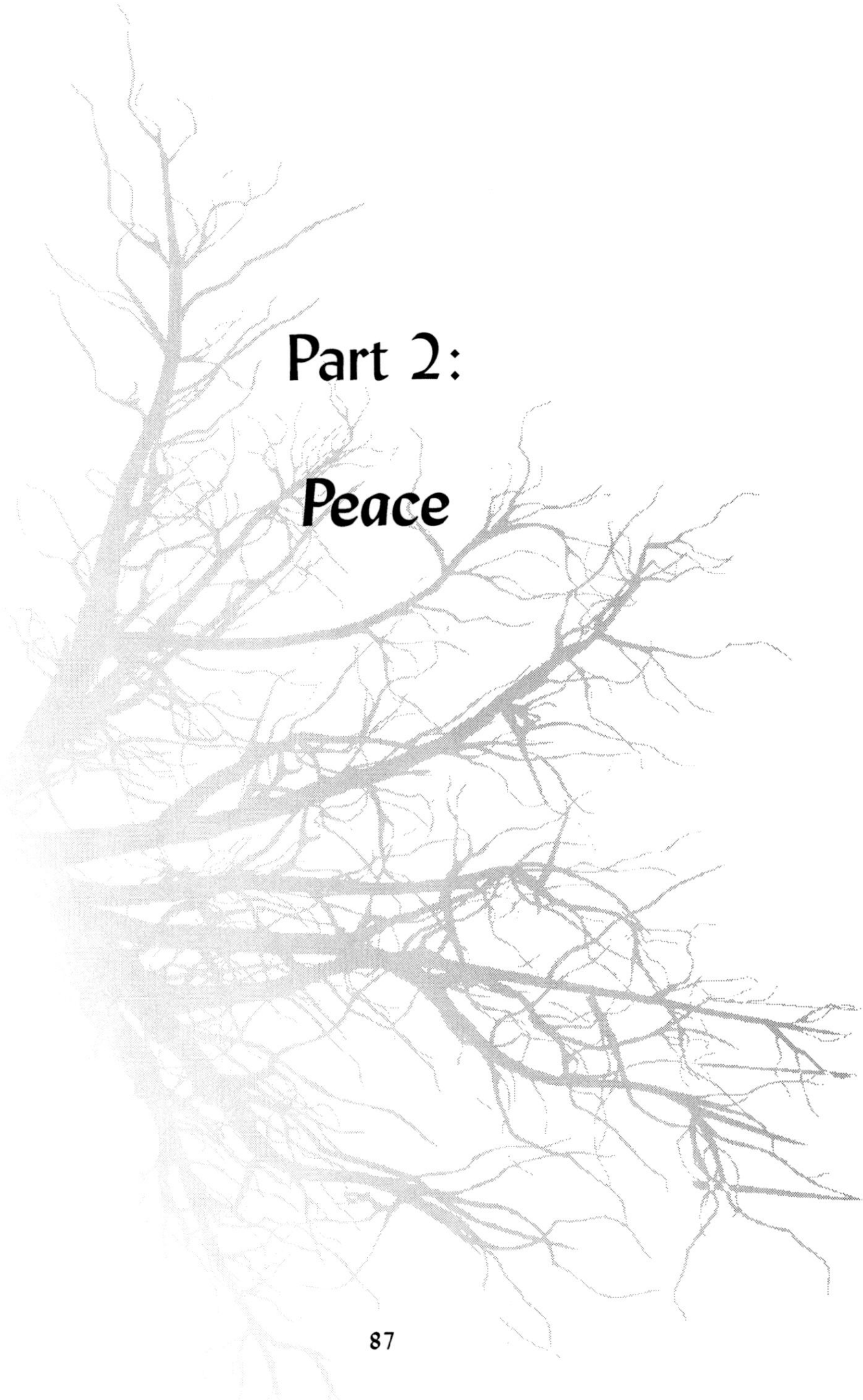

Part 2:

Peace

Chapter 18

Jean screamed in pain.

10 Years Ago

"Honey," Brandon said grabbing my hand and holding it tightly, "Just breathe. It'll be over soon. Our little baby will be here soon. I promise."

I took deep breaths like he told me. I was so happy that Brandon was here with me, but I had to focus on giving birth to our baby. I looked down at the doctor who was there waiting to guide the baby out.

"Good, good. You're doing great, Jean. I see the head crowning," she said. Brandon looked at me with such excitement, I actually kind of smiled, even during the pain.

"Our little tree is almost here!" he said while smiling. He grabbed a small towel nearby and wiped my head for me. He was too sweet. "Just keep pushing, Jean! Push! You can do this!" I took a deep breath and pushed as hard as I could. Suddenly, I felt this insane amount of pain and pressure.

"There you go!" The doctor said. "And here … HE is! It's a handsome baby boy!" she said, smiling. The baby began crying a couple of seconds later. "Congratulations!"

Brandon and I both seemed to burst out in happy tears at the same time. Our baby was finally here.

"Oh, my God!" I cried out feeling tired, but so happy. I lay back with a big sigh and looked up at the fluorescent lights on the ceiling, thanking God the baby was OK and healthy.

Brandon looked at me crying happily and leaned over, kissing my head. "You're amazing," he whispered lovingly.

The doctors wiped the baby off and wrapped him in a blanket, then laid him on my chest. He cried so loudly, but I loved the sound of it. I looked at his small face thinking, *I will never let you go.*

Brandon came as close as he could, touching the baby's head and said, "So a boy. Does that mean … " He looked at me eagerly.

I nodded. "Yeah. His name will be Joshua. Our Joshua Tree." Joshua Tree cried loudly. I imagined it was him approving his name. "Our little tree," Brandon said with a smile, happy tears falling down his cheeks.

Joshua continued to cry and scream.

Present Day

I heard Joshua's cries and screams. These weren't the same screams from when I gave birth to him though. He was screaming out in pain, and I had to help him.

My head pounded as I lay on the ground with my eyes closed. I slowly opened them, but just slightly, because I didn't want Kate to know I was conscious. I saw a terrifying scene that almost made me want to cry out, but I stopped myself.

Kate stood not far from me with her hand out in front of her. Her eyes were shining a bright white and her hand looked like it was clutching something and slowly crushing it. Then I looked over and there was Joshua, stuck up on the wall above his bed, held up by nothing, screaming in pain. It looked like as if Kate was Darth Vader or something and was using the force to kill Joshua.

This can't be real. This is insane! I thought in shock. I had to stop her. That's when I noticed the gun near Kate's foot, not too far from me. I slowly brought my hand towards it.

The pain Joshua Tree felt was excruciating as Kate held her arm up and slowly closed her hand.

I don't think I ever felt pain like this. Kate was *crushing* my soul. It actually felt like my insides were slowly cracking and on the verge of shattering. I looked at her as she killed me, her eyes glowing white—she looked like a goddess.

God! Even while she killed me, I still thought she was beautiful—talk about crazy. I have problems, I swear. That's when I heard a gunshot and the pain slightly subsided. Next to Kate stood my mom with a gun—she had shot Kate in the head.

The shot was almost exactly where Kate had shot herself previously, but Kate didn't even flinch. She looked at my mom and just slightly moved her head. My mom went flying into the wall and crumpled to the ground again.

"No!!" I screamed. Kate brought her attention back to me, the gunshot shining white and healed within a second.

Nothing is going to her stop her from killing me, I thought in fear. *This is it.*

All of a sudden, my window exploded inward. That's when *he* flew into my room through the window. It was the man from my nightmares, the man from all those years ago, the druggy with the black and red eyes. He floated in midair a couple of inches off the ground. Kate looked over at him and they made eye contact, still holding me up by my soul against the wall with her … force powers or whatever.

"Get the hell out of here, Alastair. We had a deal!" Kate yelled at the man with frustration, tightening her grip on my soul causing me to yelp.

Alastair? I thought. So that was this mans' name, but how did Kate know this?

The man chuckled and smiled slightly, floating down until his feet met the floor. His eyes flicked towards me. His irises were still that same dark black against those bloodshot eyes. They were only on me for a second, but they still made my heart stop for a brief moment, then he brought his attention back to Kate.

"Are you really that stupid?" Alastair said to her. "You really thought that I would work with you after finding out how important *he* is?" He said "he" while slightly gesturing towards me. "No, he wants more. I'm here to give him what he wants," Alastair said.

So I'm important? I thought to myself, quickly trying to put together WHY THE HELL THIS WAS ALL HAPPENING. *But who is this other "he" this Alastair guy is talking about? Who is he going to give me to?*

"Well, you can't have anything anymore. You're out of the deal. Their souls are mine and you'll have to go through me to get them," Kate told Alastair, looking away from him and at me as if the conversation was over. Even I could tell, looking at Alastair, he wasn't done.

Alastair blasted Kate with what looked like some kind of black fire from his hand. Kate screamed, as some kind of light shot out of her mouth and eyes, and then flew directly at Alastair, hitting him and blasting him out of the window.

I felt the hold on my soul lift and I fell onto my bed. Alastair went flying out of my room with the light. Kate fell onto her arms and legs, breathing hard.

Nicholas shot out of Kate's body as Alastair blasted them. She fell to her hands and knees, weak from Alastair's attack.

Damn that black fire crap hurt, Kate thought as Nicholas carried Alastair outside through the window.

His attack weakened me, but I felt my body recovering rapidly. Nicholas was gone though. I could still sense him, but he was distracted, running … or well, flying away from Alastair. Something about Nicholas not possessing me made me sad.

The *power* I sensed when Nicholas possessed me felt like nothing I ever felt before. I still had some power without him though, a lot of power actually. I could feel it running through me as I healed. But when Nicholas controlled me … it was just amazing. But now he was gone.

So maybe I'm back to myself now? I could think straight and I don't feel like killing anyone at this moment. That's when I heard Tree's voice, "Kate?"

My anger rose. "No, I'm not myself. I will never be myself again." He must be the trigger.

With him around, I'll never be myself. Joshua Tree must die.

Chapter 19

Joshua Tree got off his bed and stared at Kate on her hands and knees on the ground. She glared at the ground, her hair blocking her face. She was slightly shaking.

She should be herself now, right? I mean that light had shot out of her body, so she must have just been possessed or something.

Gosh, that felt like a crazy thing to think. But literally, Kate just came back to life after shooting herself, killed my dad, knocked my mom out twice (I really hope she's still OK), threw me against the wall by grabbing my soul with her mind, and was going to kill me. Then the druggy that tried to kill my dad and me all those years ago (and now I know his name is Alastair) flew into my room and shot Kate with some dark blast out of his hand. Then that light flew out the window, taking Alastair with it.

Nothing seemed crazy in this moment. This is the first time I have ever had a girl in my room this late at night and *this* is what happens?

"Kate?" I said questioningly, cautiously getting closer to her. I could see my parents' bodies lying on the ground in my peripheral vision, which honestly made me feel sick, but I decided to ignore them for now. I couldn't even process the fact I had lost my dad and possibly my mom, so I pushed away those feelings for at least this moment.

I knelt down in front of Kate on one knee—I kept about a foot away though. Her hair covered most of her face, but her arms were pale, like a body deprived of oxygen. "Are you OK?"

"Tree, stay away from me," Kate said through clenched teeth, sounding angry. "He's gone, but I'm not me, stay away." I was happy to hear her use my nickname though—this was her—so I got a little closer.

"Who's gone? Alastair? How did you know him? What was that light that shot out of you?" I probably shouldn't have asked so many questions, but I mean, so many were running through my head. I couldn't stop my mouth from blurting them out.

"Tree … back off," she said, sounding a bit angrier.

"Kate, it's OK. It's me." I said crawling a bit closer. "Come on. Talk to me. What happened?" I reached out and touched her arm. It was ice-cold.

"TREE!! NO!! I'm supposed to kill YOU! " she screamed and lifted her head. Her irises were glowing gray. Her face was unnaturally pale. She looked angry. I took my hand quickly away, but still knelt in front of her.

"Kill me? Why?" I asked. She lurched forward and grabbed me by my arm with her ice-cold grip, then lifted me into the air, the floor now a couple of feet under us. She held onto to me, as if I were weightless. We floated in the middle of my room for a second. I looked at her pale face and she didn't even look angry now—she looked indifferent. I looked into her glowing pale eyes and I could tell this wasn't the same Kate anymore—this was something else.

She glanced at the window and I realized what she was going to do. "Kate!! Don't even thi … "

She flew out of my window, out into the cool night, carrying me along with her.

Chapter 20

"What's going on now?" Brandon asked, his voice quavering with fear. He looked down and saw his wife's limp body on the ground.

"Jean!" I looked up and saw a chilling sight that caused me to drop the mop I was carrying. "Kate?" She stood there, with an ice-cold complexion. I saw in my peripheral view that Joshua was on his bed, but I didn't get a chance even to glance over at him, because I saw something that caused my whole body to shudder. Kate's irises turned black. She lifted her gun at me.

It's strange, the moment you realize that you're actually going to die …

I was terrified at first, but then some kind of peace came over me and I closed my eyes. I heard the gunshot and waited. There was a second of pain … then it instantly lifted, almost like it had never happened. That was it, I was dead.

You'd think I would freak out about it, but I felt … peaceful. I felt like I was asleep, but I knew I was still in Joshua's room—I could feel it. So I decided to "open my eyes," but it was more like the world came back into focus. I was floating in Joshua's room, but his room seemed brighter, lit by a white glow from above me.

I still felt like myself, but strangely … not, makes total sense—right? I wasn't a person anymore, I could tell that. I also knew I wasn't in my body, because I could see it below me, lying by the mop I was holding not long ago, blood slowly flowing around it.

I looked around the room and saw my beautiful wife lying unconscious on the ground. I could see her soul still shining brightly inside her, like a star. It shined white and purple, so pretty. I was really going to miss her.

I looked over and saw Kate fly out of the room holding Joshua by his arm, taking him with her. I could have easily followed them, but then I felt something, something powerful. I looked up and instead of seeing the ceiling, I saw the most amazing sight—it looked like space. Billions of stars were shining above me, which was why the room was brighter.

Among those millions of stars, there was one that popped out the most in the distance—it looked like the sun. I could tell it wasn't the sun though, because it shined a bright green. I felt the need to find out more about it and started to float towards the light.

Not so fast, I felt something say.

I didn't really "hear" the voice though, because I'm not sure that's how it works in death now. It was more like I felt the presence of this new being and the presence of the actual words. This seemed to cause the words to have more of an impact on me, so I couldn't move. These weren't just words here in death—they were feelings. Whatever being just uttered these words, I instantly had a feeling of what it was. This thing was demanding, scary, and it did not have good intentions.

I looked back down—I was still in Joshua's room, but there was a dark figure in here with me now. It looked like dark smoke floating on the opposite side of the room from me.

You're not going anywhere—you belong to me, it said.

Alastair flew through the air and landed on his back on the road outside Joshua Tree's house. He stood up and watched as Nicholas, in his ball of light form, flew away from him after having thrown him out the window. Alastair looked back at Joshua Tree's house.

I could go back and kill those two and collect their souls right now while Nicholas is running to recover, I considered. Then it dawned on me. *As long as Nicholas is alive, he will always be a problem. He will always get in my way. He needs to go. I can't let him get away now.* I made my decision and flew into the air after Nicholas. I wasn't going to let him get away—I was going to end him.

"Come back here, Nicholas!!" I yelled at the ball of light while he flew away up into the dark sky. It was easy to fly after him since he was in the form of a shining bright white light. It was nighttime, so he stuck out like … well, yeah, like a bright light flying through the air at night.

I flew through the cool air after him, wind howling past my ears, the air was kind of misty. I grasped at my power source and shot a dark blast at him, but missed because he went from flying upwards, to straight down.

I instantly stopped in midair, flipped around so that I was facing the ground and flew down after him—basically just falling rapidly, but using my power to fall even faster.

The light disappeared into a forest of thick trees. A second later, I fell through the branches and leaves. I flipped over, and with a huge *thud*, landed on my legs. Looking across from me, I saw the light. It slowly took the form of a man, bright white clothes forming on his body. I smirked as he formed a white long cape that fell to the ground behind him. *Stupid angel thinks he's some kind of hero—the ego!*

Nicholas stared at me with his glowing white irises. "We had a deal, Alastair! This could have gone smoothly. Shame on me though for trusting a cheating, lying, good-for-nothing demon," he said, clearly angry.

I laughed, "Oh boy, really hurt my pride there. We did have a deal, but I was told of how important Joshua Tree is, Nicholas. You basically were screwing me on this deal." He laughed this time, but it was a kind of angry laugh, obviously forced. I was getting on his nerves … awesome. I loved pushing his buttons.

"Are you kidding me? Screwing you? You didn't even know! The deal was completely fair. But no, HE had to get involved, 'cause that's what HE does. Has to stick his stupid head in everything, and you stupid demons are basically his bitches who listen to every single demand without question!" Nicholas said, his eyes shining brighter. The light began to engulf both his eyes, not just his irises. His words made me angry, but I couldn't show him that. I swallowed the anger and smiled.

"I'm his bitch? Says the angel doing everything behind his daddy's back, because he's scared of what he would do or say if he knew." I could tell he was about to explode.

"That's it. I'm done with talking," he said.

Oh yeah, here it comes, I thought to myself, smirking.

"Let's settle this," he said, floating off the ground.

I did the same. I reached for my dark power and pulled at it, causing dark vapor to flow through my body and out of me. I pushed myself at him with all my might, flying through the air, wind blowing in my ears. I went flying full speed directly at him, while he flew at full speed directly at me, too, his cape flapping behind him.

He screamed a war cry and I screamed back. He was shining a bright white light, while my darkness seeped off me.

Darkness versus light—we both yelled as we collided.

Chapter 21

Joshua Tree stared at his room window as Kate flew rapidly away from it, the new powerful Kate harshly gripping him by the arm. He flapped around like a flag, but she hung on tight.

The cold air rushed by my ears. It wasn't raining, but the air was so cool and misty, I was starting to get wet and cold—my gym shorts and shirt were getting heavy. As we got higher, I could see more of the neighborhood and I saw police lights flashing, quickly driving towards my house.

Thank God. I thought. Someone must have finally called the police. Didn't matter to me though—there was no way they could see Kate and I. She was flying faster and higher to the point that we probably looked like specks up here, plus it was too dark. My fate was in her hands now. I looked up at her. Her hair flew around rapidly in the air, her eyes focused ahead to wherever she was taking me.

"K-k-kaaaate!!" I tried yelling at her over the rushing wind and my chattering teeth, but she obviously didn't hear or just ignored me. I looked back at my neighborhood, which was getting farther away. I could see that the cops got to my house.

I really hope my mom and grandparents are OK, I thought. For a second, I thought of my dad, but I stopped. I couldn't think of him right now.

I looked straight down and my stomach flipped. Under us was a forest and we were rapidly lowering down towards it. I realized that she must be taking me to the park.

Why would she take me there? Her flying sped up with shocking speed and she went almost straight down. That's when she let go of my arm.

I realized with horror, *He must be …*

Brandon looked at the dark figure floating not far from him in Joshua's room. It took the shape of a man, but that's all. It had no face or eyes or anything, it was just a cloud-shaped man.

It laughed.

No I'm not the devil. I wish, but no. He is the reason I am here, the dark creature said to me. It had heard me.

Why do you want me? I said … or thought—hard to tell in death whether you're thinking to yourself or not—but either way, the being heard me again and responded. The devil wants you, he said simply.

I felt powerless and hopeless. I obviously had no choice in the matter—these were powerful beings. This was all bigger than me. I then noticed my wife standing under us in Joshua's room. She didn't notice us or what literally looked like the galaxy was floating above her. I guess we must be on another plane of life or something, invisible to her.

She was talking to someone. I glanced over by the door and saw her dad standing there, my dead body lying between them. I looked at my wife as she walked around my body and out of the room, her dad following. I felt some kind of strength inside of me grow after seeing her.

No, I wasn't about to let some stupid evil cloud decide my fate. You always think that when you die your soul is in the hands of God or the Devil, but I could feel that this wasn't the case. I knew where I wanted to go and what I wanted to do.

I looked up at the vast space and shining stars that replaced the ceiling. I saw the shining green one that seemed to take my attention and I willed my way towards it. I started flying towards it, when something forcefully pulled me back down.

I looked back and there was the black cloud. It hadn't moved, but I could feel that it was somehow forcing me back down, like as if there were an invisible rope pulling me back. It was so powerful, I couldn't fight it. The cloud starting reaching out and touched me. Even though I was already dead, I actually felt pain—horrible, *burning* pain.

Chapter 22

Nicholas collided with the demon, Alastair, the impact causing trees around them to sway. Weaker trees fell to the ground with loud *cracks* and *thumps*. This was a battle that had happened millions of times, an angel against a demon.

He grabbed my arms and I grabbed his. We were locked in each other's grip and staring at each other, Alastair's black eyes angrily looking into mine. His irises eerily glowed black. I felt him trying to infect me with his dark powers, trying to turn me with the same sickness that the Devil has infected all of his wretched demons. I felt this darkness trying to make its way from his hands and into my body. It felt like icy hot fire going through my veins.

I have to stop this and end this fight as quickly as I can, I thought frantically. I pushed his arms open, leaving his chest exposed, lifted myself slightly higher in the air, then kicked him full force in the chest with both of my legs. Alastair went flying back straight down into a tree, causing it to fall as he fell onto his back with a satisfying *thud.*

I flew at him, pulling at my grace inside of me—it allows me my powers—and pooled it inside my hand, causing my hand to glow. I landed right over him and he looked at me with those angry black and red eyes. He was about to move, when I blasted him in the face with my grace. White pure light flew from my hand right into his face in a continuous stream, causing his head to slam back down into the ground. I stopped the blast and then quickly kneeled down over him. He was unconscious, but I knew he wouldn't be out for long.

"All right, Alastair, let's see what you're up to." I put my hand on his head and went through his thoughts. His mind was a complete mess, full of rage and pain. I found that he was connected to another demon, which wasn't surprising—I was hoping for that actually, since I knew he had a plan. Demons usually worked together to get jobs done, so it wasn't at all surprising that he didn't tell me he was working with another demon. All they do is lie. The whole time we were "working together," I was prepared for him to betray me.

Using Alastair's memories, I found out the other demon's name, which was Lerax. I grabbed onto the connection they had to each other to keep in contact and pushed upon it. Instantly I went into the connection and was able to see through Lerax's eyes. He was talking to a bright white and red light, which was a soul. I realized this soul was Brandon, Joshua Tree's father.

I saw him start to fly away from Lerax, but Lerax stopped him by using his dark powers and pulled him back. Brandon slowly floated back and Lerax reached out to grab him.

I have to stop him. I had an idea, but I had never done it before, so I was unsure of how this would work out.

I left my human form and became only my grace, which was just a bright light, my purest form. I flew inside Alastair as if I was going to try and possess the body that he had possessed. I felt the poor soul of the human he possessed screaming out to me.

PLEASE HELP ME!! he yelled. That's not what I was here for though, so I ignored him. I felt the connection to Lerax and pushed upon it even harder.

I saw Lerax grabbing Brandon. I flew through the connection and into Lerax, so for a brief moment I was inside and part of Lerax. I ripped my way out of him, causing him to cry out in shock and pain. I was now in Joshua's room—basically what I had just done was use Lerax as a portal here.

I didn't even give Lerax a chance to react. I took my human form and lurched forward, grabbing Brandon's soul. His soul seeped into my chest and I stored him in my grace. The power another soul gave me was amazing. I turned towards Lerax and blasted him with my grace. White pure light flew from my hand and into the black cloud that was Lerax. He disappeared from existence.

Wow, I thought in amazement.

Please stop! It hurts! Let me out!! Brandon's soul yelled.

"No, I need you," I said, pushing him out of my mind.

This was the most power I had ever felt. I looked up and saw what Brandon had seen. It was the beautiful and vast space. It was amazing, but my awe disappeared quickly, replaced by hatred. This place only brought out anger from me now—it sickened me to see it again. I blinked and the ceiling returned in its place.

Alastair then came exploding into the room through the wall, blasting a huge hole in it. Outside I saw nothing but fire and death. There were policemen outside, but they were all dead, their cars wrecked and on fire. Alastair stared at me with anger.

"Give me the soul," he demanded.

Chapter 23

Jean woke up in Joshua's room and quickly got up onto her knees, thinking Kate was still in the room, but swaying from dizziness. She realized she was alone.

10 Minutes Ago

Why does my head hurt so much? I thought, feeling lightheaded. The details of what happened slowly started to come back to me—Kate coming back to life, how she knocked me out twice with her new strength, her eyes glowing and her weird force powers and how she used these powers to torture my son. I looked around and realized neither she nor Joshua were in the room anymore, but the window was now broken.

She must have taken him! I realized with shock. I stood up, still feeling lightheaded, but ignored it, turning towards the door. My stomach dropped and I stopped in my tracks.

There lay my husband with a pool of blood around him. That's when I heard the police sirens in the distance. I looked up and there was my father standing by the doorway—he was also staring at my husband's dead body. I could hear my mom bawling in the kitchen. I had to hold myself together. My dad looked at me with tears and fear in his eyes.

"What's going on?" he asked. I really wish I had a clear answer.

"Let's get out of here. We have to find Joshua," I said, holding back tears and walking past Brandon's body, avoiding the blood. I couldn't get myself to look at him like that right now.

When I walked outside with my parents, my dad holding onto my mom while she cried, the cops pulled up to our house with their sirens blaring and screeched to a stop in front of us. There were two policemen in each, one of them a woman.

A second later, an ambulance drove around the corner and stopped in front of my house, too. I looked around my neighborhood and realized there were people looking out their windows and some were even standing outside. I really wish they would all not pay attention to this.

The cops had gotten out of their cars and one of them, a cop with thick arms and about my height, walked up to me and said, "Hello, ma'am, we've been getting multiple calls around here and were told there were gunshots and screaming. Is everything OK?" I almost felt like laughing when he asked that.

Is everything OK? I looked at him and said as straight as I could, "No, my husband is dead and my son is gone." I said the words, but I put no emotion behind them. To be honest, it almost didn't even feel like me saying this.

"Is the murderer still in there?" he asked quickly, bringing his hand to the gun at his waist. I shook my head no. He didn't move his hand, but it seemed to relax slightly on the gun. "Do you know who took your son? Was it the murderer that killed your husband?"

I didn't know how to answer those questions exactly. How could I really explain the whole situation? I opened my mouth to say something, but nothing came out.

Thankfully, the cop realized he wasn't going to get any real answers out of me at this moment and said, "OK, ma'am, we're going to have a lot more questions for you, but first we'll have the paramedics get the body and then we'll have to check you all out."

I nodded, thankful to have more time to try and get my head straight. I don't think I would ever be able to think straight anymore though.

The cop pointed at my mom, who was still bawling her eyes out in my dad's arms. A woman cop with red hair walked up to them and started slowly guiding them both towards the ambulance, saying that everything was going to be OK, probably mostly to my mom. The cop with thick arms then jogged to the ambulance and told them the situation. They came out with a rolling table and body bag on top of it.

A tall cop, noticing me just standing there, came over to me and said, "Come with me, ma'am. We need to check you out at the ambulance, too. We'll start looking for your son soon though. It's going to be OK."

Every time one of them said it was "going to be OK," I almost felt like laughing. I'm not sure why, because nothing about this was funny. I felt like my world was crumbling, I lost the ones I loved the most and I had no idea how to cope.

The tall cop walked with me towards the ambulance as the paramedics with the body bag rolled quickly past us towards my house, the thick-armed cop and his partner, a bald cop, leading the way. That's when we all heard a scream of pure anger in the distance and everyone stopped in their tracks.

What now? I thought, feeling really tired. I saw the trees that were behind the houses in the cul-de-sac shortly down the road start to shake.

The cops grabbed their guns and aimed them upwards when Alastair shot out from the trees, causing my heart to feel almost like it dropped to my stomach. *He's back.*

He flew through the night sky towards us, stopped in midair and looked around, as if he was assessing the situation. The cops and everyone else around just stared in awe. He then lifted his hand and shot some kind of dark fire energy from it at the first cop car, causing it to explode and fly over our heads, landing somewhere behind us on the other side of the ambulance with a crash.

There was screaming and all the neighbors that were outside ran into their homes. Alastair shot two more blasts at both Brandon's red car and my black car in the driveway, destroying them. I jumped to the ground, scraping my arms. My dad grabbed my mom and went inside the ambulance; the two paramedics following and closing the door behind them.

The cops started shooting at Alastair, the bullets hitting him and causing blood to spew out, but he didn't even seem to mind. He then shot another dark blast at the second car, causing it to explode, too, and fly into the air. The heat was so powerful, it felt like my skin was burning. The car flew up into the air and then back down, landing on top of the red-headed lady cop and her partner, the tall cop. Their bodies were crushed under it and I swear I heard the *crunch.*

The other two cops continued firing at Alastair. He flew at thick-armed cop, grabbed his gun, crushing it in his hand, and throwing it away. Then he grabbed his head and snapped his neck, letting his corpse fall to the ground.

I cried out, unable to hold it back from the shocking gruesomeness of his attack. The bald cop quit firing his gun, realizing it wasn't doing any good, and ran at him to try and tackle him.

I had two thoughts as I watched bald cop run towards Alastair. *He is really brave*—and—*what an idiot!*

Alastair turned towards the cop and smirked. He then gave him a full punch in the stomach, causing him to fly back at least thirty feet or more, his body crumpling to the ground in front of another house, obviously dead. Next, he turned his attention to me, still lying on the road just watching all this like an idiot. I should have run away a while ago. I couldn't seem to force myself to move though. I was paralyzed with fear on the ground.

He slowly walked towards me, walking around the flaming car that had crushed the other two police. Suddenly, he stopped, noticing the ambulance. Time felt like it stood still, when I made eye contact with him. His dark irises almost seemed to glow against the red of his eyes.

"Please don't … " I begged, but it really only came out like a whimper. The ambulance door opened a crack from the back and I heard my dad's voice.

"Jean, where are you? Get in here!" he yelled.

Alastair's mouth twisted into an evil smile. He lifted his hand and shot a dark blast at the ambulance.

It exploded with the paramedics and my parents in it. I covered my head and screamed, feeling the heat from the ambulance. It tipped over and landed on its side. I couldn't look up—I was done. I closed my eyes and just prayed for this to be over.

Alastair grabbed me by the back of the neck and threw me tumbling down the road. During my flight, I hit my right arm against the ground and felt something in it *snap*. I eventually tumbled to a stop onto my back, my right arm tilted slightly at a weird angle. Alastair flew towards me and landed above where I lay. He kneeled down, grabbing me by my throat.

"I could kill you quickly," he said squeezing my throat, "but slowly would be more fun." He closed his eyes and started murmuring words that I didn't understand. I felt his hand grow warmer and then it felt like it was injecting something into my neck. Whatever he was inserting into me made its way harshly through my entire body, I groaned in pain. Finally, he let go. He stood above me and chuckled, as my body spasmed in pain.

"Haven't done that to a person in a while—doubt you'll survive. Good luck though," he said. My whole body painfully itched with what felt like bugs eating their way throughout it. The pain was so incredible, my vision started to fade in and out. One second Alastair was above me grinning, the next gone.

I heard an explosion in the distance, but I couldn't take the pain anymore and blacked out.

Chapter 24

Kate let go of Joshua Tree's arm and he fell rapidly towards the ground below, his body flipping through the air like a rag doll.

I somehow, amazingly, landed on my feet, which sounds cool, but at the same time … it was horrible. Most of my weight went onto my right leg and I felt an extremely painful *crack*. I fell onto my stomach, dizzy from the flying and the fall—the world felt like it was moving under me. I lifted my head and tried to get my bearings. I realized that basically, I was in the center of the park, lying in the middle of the huge field where kids played games or flew kites.

My right leg was obviously broken and JEEZ, was I in pain, but I had to prepare myself, because Kate wasn't done with me. I heard her land not far in front of me with a loud *thud*. I lifted myself onto my hands and knees, but that was as far as I was going to get myself up. I looked over at Kate, at least twenty feet or so away from me. She just stood there and stared at me with those gray eyes.

I quickly looked behind me as far as I could and realized the playground was to my right, so the parking lot was straight behind me. That means to my left was where our …

Kate punched me on the right side of my face, causing me to fall unto my left side. I groaned in pain, feeling my cheek starting to swell already, but was still able to find my voice.

"Please," I groaned, "you don't have to do this. I'm sorry. For whatever I did to deserve this, I'm sorry." She looked at me blankly with that ice-cold stare. I really would do anything just to get her to stop and say something.

I didn't get that. Instead, she kicked me straight in the chest, this time with that great new strength of hers. I went tumbling several feet towards the small forest near our spot. I tumbled to a stop face down on the ground and coughed out blood. That kick seemed to have probably broken a few ribs. Before I could think anymore about the pain I was in, she was next to me again, grabbing me by the back of my neck. She lifted my body and threw me into the air.

She had thrown me into the forest—it was amazing how I avoided most of the trees while flying through it. I hit the ground and went tumbling once again. I ended up landing bitterly on my back in the small clearing just before our tree. It felt like I was completely covered in cuts and blood at this point.

Above me, I saw the beautiful dark sky and stars. They were starting to fade slightly. The sun was slowly on its way. It was almost morning. I lay there in so much pain that I felt almost giddy, as if my brain was protecting me from all this pain. I actually felt like laughing, but couldn't. I struggled even to breathe at this point, because most of my ribs were probably bruised or broken.

None of this made any sense, but it was almost laughable. Why was I here? Why was the girl I liked since I was a kid beating the shit out of me? None of it made sense. Strangely, I felt some strength and I sat up slowly using my arms. She stood there, staring at me.

I looked at her beautiful gray irises. I really missed her eyes before—they used to be a friendly light brown. The ones that weren't so cold, the ones that would smile at me when I would see her in the hallway at school, the ones I slowly fell in love with, but she was still just as beautiful with the new ones. I just really missed the old Kate. Her skin was so pale now, it almost seemed to glow slightly. Unless the pain is causing me to hallucinate right now … but I'm pretty sure she's slightly glowing. She was beautiful, but deadly. She was going to kill me … I had to say something.

I groaned—it hurt to talk, but I pushed through it. "Kate … I miss you." I wanted to say more, but then I stopped. What more could I say? She stared at me with that same blank stare. It didn't seem like anything I would say would get to her. She lifted her hand slowly.

"I'm sorry," she said. I was shocked to have even heard her voice again.

She used her new force powers and grabbed my soul again. She threw me through the air until I slammed into our tree. I screamed in pain and then she released my soul. I stood with my back up against our tree, putting most of my weight against the tree and my left leg, because my right leg was useless. I coughed up more blood. My eyesight went slightly red, blood was dripping into my eyes.

Shit, I am really going to die. I looked up as a root under Kate's feet ripped itself from the ground and unattached itself from the tree, floating into her hand. It was about the size of my arm. She stared at the end of the root and it sharpened into a point. *The weapon for my execution,* I thought.

I began to really panic and looked away in fear to my right. That's when I saw it—the peace sign that I had carved into the tree all those years ago. I brought my bloody hand down and touched it.

Peace. That actually brought a slight smile to my face despite everything right now. Everything was going to be OK, no matter what. This was it, the big step that everyone had to face anyway. I was just going to have to face it kind of early—Death.

I closed my eyes, my hand on the carved peace sign on our tree's bark. I felt the bark of it on my bloody fingertips. I took as deep a breath as my broken chest would allow.

Peace. I opened my eyes and looked back at Kate. She still stared at me, as if waiting for me to be ready. The root floated slightly off her hand, the sharpened point turned to aim directly at me.

It's strange, the moment you realize you're actually going to die …

The root flew through the air and pierced its way through my chest and into my heart, then into our tree behind me, connecting me to it. The last thing I saw was her.

The world faded away from me.

Part 3:

See Me

Chapter 25

Alastair stared into Nicholas' shining white eyes with disgust, both of them floating in Joshua Tree's room. A huge hole behind him showed where he had blasted through after killing all the cops and people outside.

"Give me the soul," I demanded. Nicholas stared at me blankly, saying nothing, both his eyes fully shining a bright white, his cape slowly flapping behind him. He looked more … *powerful*—I not only could see it, but could feel it too. The shock started to settle in when I realized what he did.

"You didn't … " I said in disbelief. Nicholas stared blankly at me and simply replied, "I did."

Shit, I thought with fear.

Nicholas continued, "Brandon's soul is powering my grace. I'm as powerful as I've ever been. I'm a god, soon to be the only."

"You're killing his soul like that!"

"And why do you care? Have you grown a conscious Alastair?" Nicholas said almost jokingly, still no emotion on his face though.

"No," I replied frustrated, "I just need that soul."

"Because if you don't, your pimp will be mad?

I flew at him full speed, ready to bash his face in. Nicholas stared at me as I charged, not looking worried in the slightest. I pulled all my dark energy into my hand, about to punch him in the face, when I stopped in mid-air, unable to move, my fist only a couple of inches from his face. I didn't do this on purpose. I was frozen against my will. My whole body strained, I struggled to move any part of it. Nicholas stared at me frozen in the air, his mouth pulled up into a slight smile. My stomach dropped. He was so powerful.

"You are such an annoyance, Alastair, but just that—an annoyance. There's nothing you can do," he said, simply pushing me with a finger. I fell onto my back, paralyzed. Nicholas just floated into Joshua's room for a moment, like he was just floating in thought.

He wasn't even paying attention to me now. All of a sudden, the hole I had broken in the wall repaired itself. There were blurs of movement, which I realized were people, but everything was going backwards. I even saw myself when I had first flown into Joshua's room through the window I had smashed, but this time, I flew out backwards leaving his room, the window repairing itself.

It was like the world was on rewind.

It all eventually stopped at the point when Joshua Tree was on his knees over Kate's dead body sobbing, his mother staring at him while standing under the door frame. I looked around in confusion, only able to move my eyes.

He's ... taken us back in time?

Nicholas pulled at his grace, now more powerful than he had ever been, because of Brandon's soul, turning time back to the point where Kate Iris had committed suicide, and bringing Alastair along so that he could witness his power.

I could feel Brandon screaming from inside me in pain. Using him for this kind of task greatly harmed him. He was probably close to—well not death—but to not existing.

I stopped time to the point that Joshua Tree was on his knees, sobbing over Kate's dead body, while his mother stared from under the door frame. I stared at Kate and I knew what I had to do. I had to try and bring my daughter back from the dead.

Present Day

Kate stared at Joshua Trees' dead body with the root stabbed through his heart, pinning him to the tree. There was so much blood dripping off his body and onto the ground, slowly drying on his body.

He's dead, I thought, sending the message to Nicholas through our connection. I felt nothing in return—it seemed he hadn't even gotten the message. I felt his hold on me lessen. I could barely feel him, he felt so far away. I felt my own will becoming stronger. I stared at Tree, still feeling indifferent about him being dead.

So I'm still not who I used to be, I thought to myself. *I feel like the old Kate would have felt more emotional about the death of Tree. He was my "best friend" apparently. I guess that Kate is truly dead. What would the old Kate want to do though?* I thought.

I slowly walked up to Tree's dead body, my bare feet walking through a puddle of blood. I looked at him closely. His eyes were closed, he was all bruised and bloody from my attack. It was quite a gruesome sight.

I think the old Kate actually had feelings for him. If she had, would she ... try and bring him back? I looked at his arm and followed it down to where it was touching a part of the tree. I moved his fingers over and saw that he was slightly touching a peace sign carved into the bark of the tree.

I felt like that sign was familiar, but I couldn't bring the memory back. It seemed like a dream that you knew you had, but you couldn't fully remember it. I wanted to remember it though—I really *wanted* to remember everything, but it was so hard. I truly felt nothing now, like I was just a robot. I looked back at Tree. I looked at his face and weirdly I realized,

Yes. I want to bring him back to life.

Death is something no one understands. It's something most of us fear. Why? Because it's unknown and we all fear what we don't understand. What do we become, or do we even become anything?

Well, I guess I have some answers, because I've entered the void. Yeah, I'm actually dead at this very moment—crazy, right? How can I explain it so that you can picture it? Jeez, that's asking for a bit much, but OK.

Well, at this moment everything is dark, so I guess you can easily imagine that. Just close your eyes and that should about be what I'm experiencing right now. The tougher part to describe is what I *feel*. I feel like there is so much around me, like I'm floating, and I don't feel held down anymore by my own body—I'm free of it. Close your eyes and imagine you are a floating head. Sounds funny, I know, but that is literally how I feel.

I also know that as soon as I focus and "see" what's around me, I'll understand more. I'm just not sure that I'm ready though. All of a sudden, I feel a presence. It feels powerful, yet gentle.

Then *it* spoke to me.

I say *it,* because I'm honestly not sure whether or not this voice is female or male. It's not even one voice either. It sounds like millions of voices talking and saying the exact same thing, like a chorus. But when they spoke, it felt like the voices were all around me, inside of me and strangely—even though I guess technically, I don't have a body anymore—I felt chills run through me. These voices sounded and felt ... *beautiful.*

You are ready, Joshua Tree. I am God. See me, God said.

Chapter 26

Nicholas floated in Joshua's room, hovering over Joshua Tree as he cried over Kate's dead body. He focused his energy, preparing to use the power Brandon's soul provided him, when he came to a realization.

I'm not powerful enough to bring my daughter back to life, I realized. I pulled at my grace that contained Brandon's soul, but I can feel that it won't work. It's important to know what your powers are capable of accomplishing and I simply don't have enough power to do this. If I tried, I would fade out of existence entirely trying to do the impossible. I stare down at Kate's dead corpse, as Joshua Tree sobs over it. Strange how much he cries.

He actually had fallen for her over the years—more than I thought he would. I felt bad for him, but I quickly pushed those feelings away. I couldn't be weak—feelings cloud decisions and judgment. Besides, that crying kid would grow into a monster.

This doesn't make sense, I thought to myself, trying to think through what I was going to do. *I should be able to bring her back to life ... she came back to life before, so I should be able to do it now somehow. She has to be brought back to kill Joshua Tree.* I was as powerful as I have ever been because of Brandon's soul, yet I couldn't do a thing. I didn't understand.

I knew that if I wasn't able to bring Kate Iris back to life, this whole mission of mine was finished. I knew she had to be the one to kill him, not me.

Fate must have changed. This realization confused me as I just floated in the air, puzzled as I watched Joshua Trees' tears fall lightly on my daughter's corpse. I felt defeated.

Kate Iris paced back and forth in front Joshua Tree's body with her bloody bare feet, studying his standing corpse as his blood slowly flowed onto the ground. He was still attached to the tree with the root that she used to kill him. Seeing him like this didn't seem to bother her at all, but she knew it should. She stopped pacing and stood directly in front of him.

How can I bring him back to life? I wondered. *Doing something like that would take a lot of energy. Did Nicholas give me enough power to do that?* I did feel incredibly strong, both physically and spiritually. I walked forward, my bare feet stepping through the puddle of blood that was still collecting on the ground again, lightly putting my hand on Tree's bloody and bruised face.

The sun, now brightly above us, shined on his bloody face, yet he still felt cold. I closed my eyes and focused. I felt the new powers that Nicholas had granted me flowing through my veins and through my whole body.

The powers I never wanted. I hated him for bringing me back to life. When I died, I felt peaceful. I was done. To have been brought back was a curse. *Why did he bring me back to this horrible world?* I angrily thought. *Gosh, why do I really even care about this boy?* I looked at his stupid bloody and bruised face a little more.

I forced myself to push away that anger—wait—anger? That was an emotion right? I honestly really haven't been feeling much, but my emotions did seem to boil up a bit … because of him.

I brought my focus back to the task at hand, bringing Tree back from the dead. I didn't deserve to be brought back, but he does.

My eyes still closed, I reached into my powers—my grace is what I believe Nicholas called it—basically it seemed to be my soul. It felt strange to be able to truly feel and use the powers my soul has always possessed. Everyone has these powers, it's just like I was granted the key to open the door to them.

Reaching for them is a strange sensation to describe, too. It felt like there was strange vibration in my chest. I mentally reached for it and touched it. The vibration flew from my chest to the rest of my body. Now my whole body felt like it was vibrating, as if an electric charge were flowing through me.

I took control of this "electric" feeling and opened my eyes, the world strangely brighter than it was before. I focused, still touching Tree's face slightly. Having some kind of connection with his body would help with locating his soul and bringing it back. I push myself, reaching out into the void to try and bring him back, but my vision faltered. I fell to the ground, gasping for air, feeling dizzy and weak.

I'm not strong enough, I realized, still gasping. I struggled to bring myself back onto my feet and looked at Tree, feeling defeated. I looked at the root that had him pinned to the tree, reaching forward and touching the bit that protruded from his chest. I felt something strange from it.

It's ... slightly vibrating, too! I realize in shock. I touch the tree's trunk and definitely felt ... power. The tree seemed to be vibrating like crazy as I touched it, like a motor when you start up a car. *I can use this to bring him back to life!* I realize, beginning to feel excited and hopeful.

I'm excited? More emotions bubbling up to the surface, maybe the old Kate wasn't dead. I looked at Tree. *He's not even alive and he's helping me find myself again. I have to bring him back.*

Suddenly, I feel lightheaded again, cutting off my train of thought and falling back onto the ground. *What the hell is happening to me?* I wasn't weak from trying to bring Tree back to life this time—I hadn't even tried again yet. I looked at my hand, noticing it was slowly starting to fade.

Kate Iris slowly began to fade from existence.

Chapter 27

You may see me, God said.

I obey the millions of enchanting voices and open my eyes. Almost instantly, I had to close them again, because of how bright the light was.

Give it a moment, God said reassuringly.

I slowly open them again, my eyes began to adjust to the light … or maybe the light was adjusting for me? I'm not sure.

What I saw in front of me though made me stare in awe. It looks like an enormous, bright shining green light, though at first, it just looks like a huge wall of green light. Then I look up to see that it curves. Even when I look to my left and right, it curves in the distance. It's as if you were floating in front of the earth and see how it curves, except it's not the earth in this case, but something else entirely.

It looks like the sun, I think to myself in awe, *but I'm not burning or anything, I don't feel any heat.* I look around me and notice that I'm in what looks like space, millions of stars shining in the distance. It wasn't just your usual stars against a black night sky—it looked like galaxies in the distance, and there were so many different colors, a breathtaking sight.

You have questions, God says, with all the millions of voices in unison. Uh … duh … I hesitate, still in awe of what's taking place. I slowly collect myself—how the hell does someone talk to

God?—then I ask, *Yes … um … where am I?*

You are where the souls of every being that lives in the universe goes when Death collects them, God replies.

Goodness gracious! I ponder on that for a moment and look around at all the stars.

So … space? That's … this … is heaven?

Yes and no.

Well, that makes sense, I say sarcastically.

Here souls are able to see and do what they please—see what they want to see, and do what they want to do.

Do what we want to do, see what we want to see? Well, I kind of don't like feeling like a floating head, so I begin to picture my body—of course, with clothes, too—don't feel like talking to God naked.

I get a strange feeling and look down, seeing my body with a simple green t-shirt and dark brown pants, except I look slightly see-through, like a ghost. It's good enough though. I look back up at God and ask, *So reality isn't really a factor here?*

This is reality.

Boy … your answers are just going to give me a headache, aren't they? God actually giggled a little bit at that.

Yes, God, giggling! This was just weird in so many ways that I … I just can't … I continue with my questions.

OK, well, you … don't sound like one voice. I thought God was like … just a man or something, according to churches and stuff?

I am whatever you want me to be. I am all of you.

Wow … religion is wrong? Go figure.

They are not wrong. They're learning, trying to understand more than they can actually comprehend, like we all are.

Yeah … if you're confused, I wouldn't blame you—same here. I stare at the huge green ball of light in confusion. *Right. OK, so wait—bring it back, you're all of …*

Before I can ask God the question, a shining white and orange light appears out of the green "sun" and flies directly at me. I brace for the impact, but it just phases right through my chest and out behind me, flying off into space. I turn my head and watch it sail away, out into that vast mixture of colors. Then slowly, I turned back to the green sun … which was God.

Still crazy.

I continue to float some more in confusion for a moment, but then I begin to realize, the answer dawning on me. *You're a collection of souls, of … everyone's souls.*

Yes, I am.

Alastair stared at Nicholas floating in the middle of the room, while he lay paralyzed on his back on the ground. The only thing he could move were his black eyes, which spun around, looking at the scene before him.

I pulled at my dark energy, trying to find some way to un-paralyze myself or even leave this body I possessed, but it was useless. Whatever Nicholas did to me was too powerful to overcome—he had me locked in here. So I continue to lay only a few feet from Joshua Tree's kneeling body, crying over that girl, Kate Iris, who was dead. However, it seems that they were unable to see Nicholas and me.

It was so strange to watch Nicholas stare at Joshua Tree as he cried over Kate's corpse. *Why is he just staring at them? Why did he even bring us to this moment in time in the first place?* I thought, as I look at him floating up there. His face was blank, but I swear I saw moments where it twitched.

Did he actually look … angry? All of a sudden, I feel a presence. I start to panic, because it felt powerful, as if the whole room was … vibrating. Nothing really changed in the room though—I just *felt* something and it scared the hell out of me.

Could it be him? No, he wouldn't be here. Nicholas then glanced behind him towards his left. It seemed he was looking at something in the corner of the room. I moved my eyes towards the same corner, but couldn't see anything.

"What do you want? Who are you?" Nicholas asks the … well, the nothingness. I hear nothing in reply—shocker—but the room continued to vibrate.

Who is he talking to? I thought in confusion and, I'm not going to lie, a bit of fear. Suddenly the room stops vibrating.

"Joshua!" some woman yells. I realize the voice belongs to Joshua's stupid mother. I looked over and see Kate sitting up, her hand around Joshua Tree's throat. I look back at Nicholas, who has a smile on his face. His eyes were still shining white, but now a mix of green is in them, too.

What? So he was the one who brought her back to life?

Bringing someone back to life is no easy task. The only ones known to be able to do that were God, or Death itself.

No … if he was able to bring Kate back to life, well … maybe he is on his way to being God, I thought.

Fear truly begins to take hold of me.

Chapter 28

Nicholas stared down at his daughter's corpse as Joshua Tree sobbed over her. He couldn't help but be frustrated.

One Minute Ago

I feel … defeated. I was unable to bring her back to life. She would disappear from existence and Joshua Tree would live. This would change fate, this would change everything. I knew my daughter, Kate, was the one meant to kill Joshua Tree. Fate wasn't something you messed with—as an angel, I knew that.

I guess I'll have to kill him myself, I thought with frustration. The act of changing fate could possibly end time itself, but I couldn't let him live. His very existence would also threaten the universe and all who lived in it, so I was willing to take my chances. I pull at my grace, causing Brandon to scream with pain inside me, preparing to kill Joshua Tree.

Suddenly I feel the presence of … God? It was hard to tell if it was actually God or not, but the room almost felt like it was … vibrating.

Whatever it was, it was a powerful being. I feel the presence behind me. I look over to my left to the corner of the room behind me and see a haze of green light. It looks like green water vapor. In that haze, I could slightly see someone standing in it, but couldn't make out a face or anything.

"What do you want? Who are you?" I asked the Being. I could tell this wasn't God—it couldn't be—*right?*

I got no reply. Instead, the room stops vibrating and I feel this overwhelming power take hold of me. It feels like the presence was inside me, but not possessing me, more like providing my grace with … almost unlimited power. I look down at Kate and instantly know what to do—I use that power. I brought Kate back to life with a simple thought, triggering the curse I had laid upon her as a baby.

She was mine—no longer human—no more emotions to cloud her judgment. I knew she had grown a fondness for Joshua Tree over the years. I knew they were meant to meet, that's why I impregnated her mother in the first place, but I was surprised that she was able to find him actually so young. The curse upon her soul had activated the day she met him. Now it was in full affect and Kate Iris was powerful enough to be rid of Joshua Tree. Fate was back on course.

I pull her soul back into her body and the curse infected it. She opened her eyes, revealing her gray irises again. She was no longer fully human. She was almost as powerful as an angel. I knew that maybe one day she would be even more powerful than an angel—of course—she was my daughter.

She's beautiful. I thought, smiling.

"Joshua!!" Joshua Tree's mother yells. Kate sat up and grabbed his throat. My job now done, I use this almighty power to bring Alastair and me back to the present, back to Joshua Tree's empty room with the huge hole Alastair had blown in the wall. I unparalyzed Alastair and he quickly stands up.

"So *you* were the one who brought Kate back to life?" he asked, pointing up at me. I could clearly see the fear in his black and red eyes.

"Yes, I am God." I replied looking down at him from the air, the new power still flowing through me. "I was going to let you live to tell everyone of my presence, but I'm not feeling as kind anymore. You are no longer needed. Goodbye for good, Alastair."

I lift my hand to extinguish him from existence, when I notice that the green haze has disappeared from the corner. The power instantly leaves me and I feel weak, like when you have a sugar rush and then crash, except on a whole different level. I fall down from the air and onto my hands and knees. I try to feel for Brandon's soul but that was also gone—he was no longer stored in my grace.

Where did he go? My grace was still with me, but I feel so weak. I had used too much power from it and was drained. It would take a long time for my grace to heal and get my strength back. *What has happened to me? Why would that being give me powers just to take them away?*

I look up and Alastair has a big grin on his face. "What's happened God?" the demon said while chuckling. He walked towards me, his black irises glowing against the red of his eyes.

He was angry, and I was powerless.

Chapter 29

Joshua Tree slowly turned himself away from the huge green sun that called itself God. He looked across what he now knew was truly the universe, which was everything. It was beautiful, all the colors and bright lights made by the stars and galaxies. All the different worlds out there made him feel so small just floating around, looking at it all. A white and blue star slowly flew by him; science says that stars are just gas, but he could tell that's not what this was.

T*his is a soul isn't it? Wait, all the "stars" are souls,* I thought to myself.

The white and blue light stopped in front of me and started to take the shape of a woman. She looked at me when she was in full form, a blue and white light in the shape of a woman.

She nodded at me, as if confirming what I had just thought. She reached her hand out and I got the urge to do the same, so I did. I slightly touched her fingers, feeling … well I'm not sure what. My fingers faded right through hers, so I didn't physically feel anything, but I did feel this warmth inside me—love, I believe—real love.

Thank you, I said to her. It felt like this was simply a gift of some kind.

She slowly took her hand away, a smile on her face, turning back into a ball of blue and white light, and then floated away from me. I could only feel traces of the warmth that she had given me as she left. I watch in awe as the soul floats away, my hand still extended in front of me. The ball of light quickly changes course and flies behind me. I glance behind me at God and saw the light fly into the big ball of green light, fusing and becoming one with God.

So I can do almost anything here? I thought to myself, turning back to the vast universe.

Yes, you can. The millions of voices of God responded, taking me by surprise. I just meant to think that to myself, but again, I forgot that this was God—they could probably hear everything.

Sorry, I'll try and give you more privacy, God said.

I decided to actually try and "talk" this time, realizing we've been talking mentally this whole time. Since I could do anything here, I figured it was possible, even though clearly there was no air and I was dead—whatever—worth a shot. I cleared my throat with a slight cough, taking myself by surprise.

"No, it's OK," I said, taking myself by surprise again. Felt like I hadn't actually talked in a long time and it was strange hearing my voice, "You're God. You can't help it." I felt God actually become amused by that reply. I stared off at the billions of stars, which I now knew were also billions of souls out there. I shook my head in disbelief. It was such a huge universe, and here I was, floating in front of the *one* who knew the answers to it all.

"This can't be real. This must be like … well, this is the kind of stuff that only happens in movies or TV … or in a book."

You are in a book.

"What?"

This is a story that will be written. Or probably is already written. Time works differently here.

"By who? You?"

I guess you could say that. I technically do all.

"That's ... crazy ... I'm in a book? See, I feel I've heard this before or, well, seen it before on that one show, *Supernatural.*"

Yep. Good show.

"Well, yeah, this feels similar."

Everything is connected Joshua Tree. I feel inspiration would be a good word to use here. Even your name ... it's connected to other things; inspired by other things.

"My name? ... OK, you know what? I'll just move on, because honestly, my head can't wrap around this."

I understand. It is a lot to take in.

My head was basically hurting after that. Someone else could be reading this "story" right now in a book? Could this ever be a movie?

I hope not, God said. *Movies are never as great as the books.*

"Really? What happened to giving me and my thoughts some privacy?"

Sorry ... technically, it wasn't your "thoughts" ... wasn't in the italics.

"What?"

Never mind. Forget it.

I continued to stare out into the universe, thinking about how to get my head around *any* of this somehow.

"So I'm dead? This is it then? I'm just going to be here for the rest of time?" I asked, feeling slightly saddened. This view of the universe was beautiful and I guess I could go wherever I want and do whatever I want, but I knew it would never be the same as life. I felt like I wasn't ready to be here, I felt like I wasn't done.

No. Your feelings are correct, you're not done.

"Oh, so you're going to bring me back to life?" I asked excitedly, turning myself back around to look at God.

Yes … and no.

"There you go again making sense," I said sarcastically.

You will be brought back to life, but not necessarily by me. Now before you ask any more questions, you must let me talk, since we are running out of time, God said more urgently.

My stomach kind of flipped with how straightforward God sounded now. What time limit were we on? Why so urgent?

Every creation has a purpose. Every soul is important, with their own purpose, their own power. There are billions of people on Earth, a child born every day, yet each soul created is unique in its own way. It truly is a beautiful thing Joshua Tree, and yet almost seems impossible. The way the world works would be like a flower that has petals that are all unique in their own way. Every petal a different color—when you see it you think that it's strange, yet beautiful.

The voices of God spoke with such passion, I feel overwhelmed. I am actually able to feel what God feels, like the emotions are radiating off this being, it almost hurts. There are so many different emotions from all the souls: sadness, excitement, awe, anger, joy. I almost feel like screaming to tell them to stop, but I hold back and let God continue the speech.

Joshua Tree … you have a great purpose. Dark times are coming and I believe that you will have an important part in the chaos to come. But I am unsure whether you will stop it, or be the cause of it.

That caught me off guard.

"What? How could you be *unsure*? You're God!" There was no response for a bit, making me really uncomfortable. This almost felt like when my dad had talked to me in the car about making choices. Both my dad *and God* didn't trust me to make the right choices?

"OK … well ... I promise I don't mean to … well, I don't know … do anything bad. I just … I still don't understand though. What do I do if I'm the problem? What do I do to cause all of this 'chaos'?"

God doesn't reply again. I just stare at the big ball of green light, eager for a response. This was so stupid—how the hell is my existence this important? Gosh, if this is a book, I'm sorry—it's probably a terrible one.

I sighed in frustration thinking God has stopped talking to me, when all of a sudden, the voices reply,

You may be the one who kills me.

Chapter 30

Jean opened her eyes and stared at the blue sky, the sun just making its way across it, scraps of metal and glass lying all around her from Alastair's attack. Her body shook with pain.

Please make this pain stop, I begged my body. I was in so much pain, I continued to shake and spasm. The pain was not just from my cuts and bruises though. It was because Alastair had touched me, infecting me with something that was slowly killing me.

I could feel that whatever he had injected into me was crawling throughout my body, almost like it was a small animal ripping through my insides. My eyesight kept fading in and out from the pain, but I was able to stay conscious.

I looked over and saw the ambulance that was destroyed, on its side, still on fire on the inside. That had my parents inside of it. They were gone.

I swear if I live … I'll hunt that demon down and destroy him. I thought with anger. My insides suddenly felt like they were literally on fire and I screamed in pain, getting into the fetal position.

If I live.

I knew this was it. I could feel myself dying. I was kind of grateful though, the pain was unbearable, but slowly subsiding as I gave in to death. Maybe now I would go see my husband,

Brandon Tree. The thought of seeing him was nice. My son, Joshua Tree … well I just hoped he was OK wherever he was.

I'll miss that kid. I let out my last breath, letting death take me away from my body and pain.

Alastair chuckled as he walked towards Nicholas. It was the middle of the day now, so the sun was shining behind Alastair through the hole he had created in Joshua Tree's room.

This has really been a long day, Nicholas thought to himself, feeling weak and tired.

"How the tables have turned," Alastair said through his chuckles. I tried to crawl away from him on my hands and knees towards the door behind me, but he stepped on my cape, stopping me.

"Why the hell do you even have a cape? Who do you think you are—Superman?" He then grabbed my cape and swung me through the air, doing a whole 360 turn, throwing me at the wall next to the door. I went slamming into the wall back-first. He had thrown me so hard, I stuck into it.

He flew at me and grabbed me by the throat, pulling me out of the wall and throwing my body face down on the ground. I slammed into the ground and lay there flat on my stomach. I wanted to turn into my grace and fly away, but I was too exhausted and beaten. He knelt down in front of me, grabbing me by the hair on the back of my head with his right hand, lifting my head by it. He then took out a knife from his back pocket with his left hand.

A knife? He can't kill me with this, I thought. Then I noticed the carvings on the metal and on the black handle of it. Alastair must have realized I noticed the carvings, because he laughed, putting it against my throat.

"That's right, mister all-and-powerful-angel, a knife that can kill you. Now give me the soul!" he yelled, slightly grazing the knife on my throat. The cut burned, causing some of my grace to leak out of the cut, floating into the air and fading away like white vapor. I looked at him kneeling in front of me—he was only a shadow, the sun shining behind him through the hole in the wall. His black irises glowed, so they were almost the only thing I could see. I struggled to reply, "It's ... gone. I know you must have felt that ... *Being* earlier, too. It took it."

"Well, how convenient! What was that thing anyways?"

"I don't know."

"You lie! Give me the soul!"

"If I still had it, wouldn't you think I would have used the power against you by now? That *Being* took it from me."

He pushed the knife harder, cutting my throat a bit more. More of my grace flowed out of the cut, so I began feeling light-headed. Suddenly I heard a weird screech of some kind.

Alastair yelled out in pain, dropping the knife with a clang onto the ground, and letting go of my hair. He stood up and I saw something on his back. It quickly jumped off though. I got up as fast as I could onto my knees.

Alastair turned around and I saw a bite mark on the back of his neck, blood from the possessed body flowing out. Alastair's dark energy also slowly seeped from the wound, flowing into the air and disappearing like smoke.

His dark energy ... that's strange ... I looked to see what attacked Alastair. There, across from him, stood Joshua Tree's mother, Jean Tree. Or at least what I assumed was her.

The first thing I noticed were her eyes. Her irises were purple and she was covered in blood. There was even blood completely around her mouth. She smiled, revealing rows of sharp teeth between her normal teeth on the bottom and top of her gums. Blood dripped down her chin. *A lot* of blood dripped down her chin—Alastair wasn't the only one she had bitten.

"This is impossible! No human has ever survived that curse!" Alastair yelled in shock.

"Alastair what did you do!?" I yelled at him. Jean then took her eyes off him, looking at me with those piercing purple irises. She still smiled with those chilling sharp teeth, then said in a raspy voice, "He created a monster." She looked back at Alastair and jumped towards him, ready to kill.

Chapter 31

Kate lay under the tree next to Joshua Tree's corpse, which was still pinned against their tree. His body stood there, with blood slowly dripping off it. Kate lay on the ground gasping for air, her body still flickering in and out of existence.

I lifted my hand and looked at it as it slowly became translucent and then solid again. My body kept fluctuating from feeling weak and back to normal, so much that I threw up onto the ground. I couldn't comprehend how I was feeling, but I felt like I was just … fading. All of a sudden … it just stopped.

My head still pounded from whatever my body had just experienced, but I generally felt better. I stayed on the ground for a bit longer though, not trusting myself to stand up.

What the hell is happening to me? I thought to myself while lying on the ground. Suddenly I felt Nicholas's connection to me come back stronger than ever—it shocked me so much, I stopped breathing for a moment. He felt so strong! Then a few seconds later, almost like a switch, he lost that power and the connection weakened. He was distracted and not paying attention to me. *Thank God,* I thought, grateful for some more time.

I decided I had to move quickly and stood up, hoping my body would stay put. I put one hand on the tree, feeling the power flow through it and into me, and had my other hand on Tree's corpse. I closed my eyes, letting the power from the tree flow throughout my body, providing my grace with enough power to bring Joshua Tree back to life … I hoped. There was so much I could do with this power, but I had an objective, so I pushed away those dark thoughts and focused on finding his soul.

My soul felt like it stretched out of my body, shifting through the void, searching for Joshua Tree's soul. Every soul gives out a different feeling into the universe. There were billions of souls in the universe; I could sense each one as I made my way through the void. So you'd think this would take forever to find one specific soul, which I thought for a moment too, but using the power this tree provided, I was able to narrow it down quickly, sensing Tree's soul.

Kate? I felt Tree's soul say, confused when he sensed my presence.

Come on, I replied, pulling on his soul to bring him back to his body.

You may be the one who kills me, God said to Joshua Tree.

"What? How is that even possible? How can you die? How could I even do that?" Joshua Tree asked in shock.

I'm not even sure, but this could be a possibility, if fate continues in its present direction. That is why I tell you this, it's why I am talking with you now, and will be working with you. I believe we can make things right. I'm going to give you powers, Joshua Tree.

"Oh, wow, Powers? Like … you know … super-hero nonsense?"

… Sure, super-hero nonsense.

"Will I get a suit?"

Maybe.

"Whaaaaattt?"

We can discuss that later though. For now, I will just provide you with powers. One of them will be the ability to bring people back to life.

"Whaaat? I'll be able to bring anyone back from the dead?"

Yes and no.

" .... Yes and no—do you even realize how that answers nothing when you say that?"

I have rules because I can't have you messing with the order of things. Bringing a soul back into the world is an extremely powerful ability, which I only allow on the rarest occasions. Allowing you these powers, even with rules, is still dangerous, but I believe is necessary because of the circumstances to come; so you will only be able to do this when I allow it and you are only allowed to bring back three people from the dead.

A thought instantly came to my head. "Kate … when she died in front of me … "

Instantly the universe faded around me into darkness, then I was in the corner of my room shrouded in a green mist. Through the mist, I saw myself, from the past, kneeling over Kate's dead body with the gun wound in her head. I stared at my past self, sobbing over her body. The memory of that moment made my heart ache. I came to a realization.

"So even though this was in the past, I can bring her back?"

Yes, time doesn't necessarily affect me. It also doesn't affect you when you are in my presence. Time and the path it takes gets a bit more complicated when you're with me.

"Wow … that is surprising, because nothing is complicated with you."

I can also bend and turn it any way I'd like. When you're with me, you're basically not even affected by time.

"Huh—OK, so if I'm thinking about this the right way, I was the one that brought her back at this point?"

Yes.

"Wowza, this is some *Back to the Future* nonsense going on here. OK, well, I also remember that when she comes back she, like, *changes*."

Correct.

"Why does she change though? Can I stop that from happening?"

I felt the voices of God grow uneasy. I could feel that they knew how much she meant to me. I could tell I wasn't going to like what they were going to say.

Sometimes when you bring someone back to life, there is a consequence, Joshua Tree. You can't always just bring someone back to life without a consequence. In this case, you know what happens to Kate Iris ... do you still want to bring her back?

"But why does that happen? I still don't understand. Why does she change?"

There was a flash of a bright light. A man with white hair, white clothes, and even a freaking white cape formed out of that light and floated above my past self and Kate's dead corpse.

"Well, this definitely didn't happen," I said looking at my past self, seeing if he noticed this white guy floating above him, but there was no reaction. My past self didn't notice and neither did my mom over at the door. I looked back up at him, recognizing him.

"That's the man I saw in the woods yesterday. Who is he?"

That is Nicholas. He is an angel.

"So he works for you?"

No, he used to. I felt a bit of anger in those words from God. *Now he wants to kill you, Joshua Tree.*

"Huh?"

I know you want to know why, but there just isn't time to explain.

"I thought time wasn't a factor for you? What's the rush?" I said, kind of joking, but kind of not. God ignored my comment anyways.

What I can say is that he is the reason Kate changes. To bring her back, we must use him as a vessel. We cannot intervene with this moment of time ourselves or risk too many problems. So do you want to bring Kate back to life?

Something caught my eye in my peripheral. I looked over and saw the demon whose name I believe was Alastair, remembering that Kate had called him that. He was lying on the ground, not moving, which I found odd.

I looked back at Kate's dead body, blood flowing all around her head. A memory flashed in my head. I saw her laughing under our tree. Quickly, as fast as it came, the memory was gone. A tear fell down my cheek. Even knowing what she became, I couldn't just let her die—maybe I could help her in time—help her remember who she used to be.

"Yes, I want to bring her back."

OK, God said. With that, I felt this amazing power that overwhelmed my mind to the point that it actually hurt. I fell to one knee with my eyes closed. There was so much information about the world given to me within seconds. I felt so much power I could tell that I could destroy this world with just a thought. It would be so simple. I felt the room begin to vibrate because of me. I could destroy everything, every molecule, every atom for miles.

Relax, God said, don't let the power consume you.

"I'm ... trying!" I screamed. I stood up as much as I could and put my hands to my head to try and focus.

"What do you want? Who are you?" I heard Nicholas ask in my direction. I guess he was able to sense my presence now. I opened my eyes, the world a bright green now.

Relax, God repeated.

I took a deep breath and stood up straighter, taking control by focusing on the task at hand, bringing Kate back to life. The room stopped vibrating, as I began to focus my power. Nicholas was looking at me, but I could tell he couldn't completely see or hear me. I felt hatred towards Nicholas ... I knew him ... all this knowledge told me that I did... I pushed the thoughts aside for now. *I have to focus*, I thought to myself.

"OK, I can do this. How do I bring her back to life?" I asked God, determined.

Provide the power to Nicholas. He must be the one to bring her back.

I wanted to argue, but I could feel there wasn't time and that God was right. I just *knew* he was right and that it was the only way. I hated that. I also feel you actually reading these words right now ... holy crap, I am a book ... jeez, I have to focus.

I was so powerful, yet at the same time, powerless to fate. If I brought her back to life myself ... the world could possibly end because of like, you know, the butterfly effect kind of deal. So dramatic, I know. OK, the world wouldn't end, but a lot could go wrong.

It's a sad truth—you cannot control everything, even with the power of God. Now provide him with the power.

With a simple thought, I regrettably provided Nicholas with the power to bring Kate back to life. I hated doing this—it felt like I was helping the enemy in a way. When I gave his grace the power, I was able to read his mind for a moment.

Kate is his daughter, I realized in shock. I couldn't believe it—how could Kate be the daughter of an angel?

Nicholas looked down at Kate and I could feel his joy. He used the power—I felt him bring her back, triggering a curse that was laid upon her soul. It made me so angry that there was nothing I could do in this moment to undo this curse. He put Kate's soul back into her body and she opened her eyes. Her irises were that cold gray that brought chills down my spine.

"Joshua!" yelled my mother, who was still under the door frame. Kate got up and grabbed my past self's throat. I looked away from the familiar scene and saw Nicholas disappear, taking Alastair with him.

With just a simple thought, I followed them.

Chapter 32

Almost nothing changed. Joshua Tree appeared in the corner of his room, still slightly shrouded in a green mist. However, this time no one was in here accept for Nicholas, Alastair, and him.

"We're in the same place, but just at a different point in time," I said.

Correct, the voices of God replied. I looked around my room and noticed that to my left there was a huge hole in my wall.

"Jeez, well, that hole will be hard to live with."

You're not going to live here anymore, God said, these events have changed everything.

"I know, I figured, just kind of joking."

I looked back at Nicholas who was still floating in the middle of my room. Alastair was now unparalyzed and standing. They were talking to each other, but I didn't really care what they were saying. I tuned them out because I felt another soul inside Nicholas, which I hadn't noticed at first. It was in pain. *Help me!* the soul screamed, feeling my presence as I sensed it. I recognized the sound and feeling of the soul.

"Dad ... " I whispered in shock. Anger pulsed through my being. Nicholas was using my dad for his own agenda. He was torturing his soul, using and abusing it. " ... you son of a bitch," I screamed as I ripped my father's soul out of Nicholas. It flew out of him in the form of a white and red translucent light and into my hand. I then ripped my powers out of Nicholas, too—he fell to the ground, weak.

I smirked as Alastair walked towards him with a smile on his face. He deserved what was coming to him for torturing my dad. With that, my room faded away and I was floating in space again, with God in front of me. I looked down at the white and red light in my hand, which was my dad's soul.

"Hey, Dad, your soul looks pretty cool," I said with a smile.

Hey ... little tree. And not surprising, been working out, he said weakly. He was OK though, I could tell because of the humor.

"Don't get cocky now," I said chuckling. "Dad … I could bring you back to life," I said, realizing it basically as I said it.

You have to know your options, Joshua Tree, God interrupted. I feel that this is important for you to know. Your grandparents have died, and so has your mom.

I looked up at God in shock, unable to say anything. I looked back down at my dad's soul, feeling his sadness, too.

"So I have to decide—I have to decide who to save in my family." My eyes began to water up with emotion. This was all too much. An idea dawned on me and I pushed away my sadness, no time. I replaced it with determination.

"Let's go to before my mom and grandparents die! So instead of having to bring them back to life, I can just stop them from ever dying!"

That can't be done.

Are you kidding me? Why were there so many rules here? I was starting to grow tired of them. "Are freaking you kidding me? YOU JUST SAID that time wasn't a factor around you, that you can bend it and crap."

But fate is. They were supposed to die. The only option you have is who you want to bring back to life. You can save your father and two others.

"No, I'm not going to let … "

Little tree, my dad said, interrupting me. *I want to make this easier on you. Let me go.*

"Dad … no … "

Joshua listen, I'm tired. If you brought me back like this, I'm not sure I'd ever be the same. I need to rest. Go save your mother and them. I'm OK. I'll be fine. I really need to rest.

I nodded—I could feel that he was weak. This just wasn't fair though.

"I'm sorry for what that damn angel did to you, Dad … I'll miss you."

I'll miss you, too. But don't worry, I'm not that far.

"Such a cliché thing to say, Dad. Forgot to say you'll be in my heart," I said sniffling, letting one tear escape my eye.

He chuckled, *Hey, I'm dead; I'm allowed to be cliché. Take care of Mom. And remember, I love you, no matter what you do, little tree.*

I nodded. "I promise. I'll keep Mom safe."

With that I lifted my hand and let go of his soul. The white and red light flew out of my hand and towards God, fusing into the green sun. I took a deep breath and let it out.

"OK, let's go save my mom," I said determined. With that, I disappeared from space.

Chapter 33

Joshua Tree appeared on the road facing his house and was overwhelmed by the destruction all around him. It was hard to see the house and neighborhood he had lived in all these years be thrown into so much destruction.

Is this my fault? he thought to himself as one of his neighbors sped right through him in their car and out of the neighborhood. It was the neighbors from a few houses down.

I didn't really know the adults who lived there—think they had a boring last name like Johnsons or something, easy to forget—but I knew their daughter, Kimberly. She was only six and I had to babysit her one day. She was a nice girl; I hope they are leaving for good now though. It's too dangerous here now obviously. I bet the whole neighborhood will be moving out after this.

I held my breath for a moment and released it slowly, trying not to let the scene get to me too much. To my left was an ambulance on its side, destroyed and still on fire. In the front lawn was a cop car flipped upside down and I could tell there were people smashed under it, because of the puddle of blood and guts that was splattered around it. Blood, glass, and metal was everywhere.

Directly in front of me on the side of the road lay my mom in the fetal position—she was dead. I could tell even from a distance, because … well, because being "dead" too lets you feel everything a bit deeper I guess. It sounds cheesy in a way, but sometimes the truth is cheesy. I could feel that her soul was gone and that this was just an empty corpse.

I ran towards her and knelt over her. Seeing her like this just … destroyed me. My eyes began to water up. I put my hand on her shoulder, surprised that I could feel her. My hand didn't phase through her or anything.

"Mom … " I said, a tear falling down my cheek. I moved her shoulder, as if trying to wake her up. "Mom … I need you … I don't know what's happening … "

Joshua Tree, God said lovingly, you can bring her back …

I wiped my cheek. That would have lifted my spirits, but I knew that there was a catch, I could feel it. Something was wrong with the way she died.

"What's wrong with her?" I asked, as a couple more tears fell down my face. I wiped them away and tried to control myself. God sighed.

Alastair has infected her soul. You can bring her back, but she wouldn't be the same. She would struggle. She would have … a hunger.

"A hunger? For what?"

This spell is different from anything that has been used before. From what I can decipher right now … blood at first … it could grow worse though …

"A vampire? Those are real?"

She'd be related to them, yes. This curse though … it's strange. It's different.

"Both Alastair and Nicholas have infected my mom *and* Kate's soul," I said with no emotion. I knew I was angry but I couldn't feel it at the moment—I was saving it for another time. So this is what it felt like to want revenge on people.

Sirens blared in the distance causing me to look up—more cops on their way I guess. I looked back down at my mom lying on her side in the fetal position. She looked like she was just sleeping, peaceful. This was such a hard decision. Bringing her back would be such a selfish act. I didn't know what she would come back as—if she would be like Kate, or worse. A hunger for blood, she'd be a monster …

Words echoed in my head: *Take care of Mom,* my dad had said. Would bringing her back be what he would want?

You're running out of time, Joshua Tree, God said urgently.

I nodded. Two more cop cars suddenly drove around the corner and stopped just before the ambulance that was on its side. Four cops got out, two in each car, and took out their guns. I looked at them and could feel their fear. They couldn't see me, but they saw this scene around my house. God was beginning to provide me with the power. I felt it overwhelming me.

"OK, I'll bring her back," I said making the decision. With that, I stood and closed my eyes. There was no need for a vessel this time it seemed. I didn't understand how any of this worked, but I didn't really care—it was the power of God, for God's sakes. There was so much to question, why really think about it right now?

I felt her soul as I grabbed it from the void, so I could feel that it was infected. I felt some of my own regret as I pulled it out of the void and back into her body. As I opened my eyes, her body started to shake—that's when the cops finally noticed her, aiming their guns at her shaking body. One of them slowly made their way over to her.

The cop that walked towards her was an Asian man with black hair. His name was Jonathon Lang, he had two kids; a son in the 5th grade and a girl that was only four years old. He had a wife named Kaitlin whom he truly loved. She was a white woman with light-brown hair and had cancer. She was in the hospital at this very moment. Jonathon always had her in the back of his mind.

"What the hell? Why do I know this?" I asked, realizing there was no way I could have known this. I didn't know this man at all, but the information of his life seemed just to be there in my head as I looked at him.

To bring people back to life, I must provide you with my power, so this also brings my knowledge. This is what being God is—knowing all.

I looked at Jonathan and had a sickening feeling as more information presented itself to me. "He's going to die … " I said in shock. I just … knew.

Yes, he is.

"And I can't stop it."

No, you can't

Chapter 34

Joshua Tree's mom screamed and opened her eyes. Her irises were purple—the infection upon her soul had taken full effect.

She was no longer my mother. She quickly got up with unnatural speed. Jonathon Lang had no time to use his gun as she hit it out of his hand and it went flying away as she tackled him to the ground. He screamed for his life as my mom opened her mouth, revealing sharp teeth between her normal teeth on both the top and bottom of her mouth, almost like a shark. She bit into Jonathon's neck, sucking his blood.

I ran forward, getting ready to rip her off him, but I instantly stopped, against my will—I was paralyzed. "What the hell? Why can't I move? I have to save him! I have to stop her!" I yelled.

There are things that shouldn't be interfered with Joshua Tree. This is one of them. I'm sorry.

Jonathon screamed as she sucked the life out of him.

"OK, this is getting ridiculous! He's dying here!"

This is what it means to be God.

His screams turned into gurgling. I fought to try and move, but couldn't.

You cannot always interfere. You must let fate take its course.

The gurgling became whimpers.

"Let fate take its course? Screw fate! I brought her back to life—I interfered then! Jonathon is dying because of my choice!" I screamed, struggling to move.

His whimpers became silence.

I'm sorry, the voices of God said.

I watched as Jonathon Lang died in front of me.

The other cops saw my mom on top of Jonathon and instantly started shooting at her. Some of the bullets hit her in the shoulder, but she quickly jumped up into the air and ran at the other three cops, leaving Jonathon's corpse and easily avoiding their bullets with her supernatural speed. She moved like a predator after prey. I just stood here, watching and helpless, as my mom murdered these cops with ease, too.

She ran at one of the cops, grabbing a large sharp piece of glass off the ground and threw it into the heart of one of them, instantly killing him. She then tackled a woman cop, biting into her neck, ripping off a chunk of it. The female cop screamed in pain, which gurgled into silence. The last male cop continued to shoot at my mom, bullets hitting her, but seeming to have no effect. She spit out the chunk of this woman's neck and then jumped at the last cop, grabbing his neck and snapping it, killing him. His body crumpled to the ground. She had just killed three cops in seconds … but I felt like I had killed them. I was the one who had unleashed this monster.

I looked back down at Jonathon, his empty eyes staring into the blue sky. I stared at him as my mom started to suck on the blood of her fresh kills. I looked over at the ambulance that was on its side.

Your grandparents are in there. You only can bring one more person back to life. You can only choose one of them, God told me.

I looked back down at Jonathon and sighed.

"I'm sorry Grandma, Grandpa, but I think you guys would

agree with this decision." I closed my eyes and let the overwhelming power of God vibrate through my being. With what seemed to be a simple thought, I brought Jonathon Lang back to life. He closed his eyes and opened them again, the light of life filling them again.

I sighed with relief, no catch this time—this was just regular Jonathon Lang. He stood up and looked around in shock. He quickly located his gun and ran to it a few yards away, picking it up. He then aimed it at my mom, who was still sucking blood from a body on the ground.

"No wait!" I yelled, which was pointless because he obviously couldn't hear me.

He shot at my mom and it hit her in her back shoulder, which healed back up in seconds, faster than it had before. The blood she was drinking was making her stronger. I knew she would be fine though … it wasn't her I was worried about.

She looked up from the corpse from which she was sucking blood and growled angrily, blood oozing out of her mouth. She then ran at Jonathon with her supernatural speed, eager to kill him again.

"NO!" I yelled. I ran forward, surprised that I could actually move again. I ran in front of Jonathon and lifted my hand as my mom jumped towards us. This was probably a dumb idea.

A green translucent force field exploded from my hand and surrounded both me and Jonathon like a bubble. My mom jumped into it, unable to stop her momentum, and went flying backwards onto her back. She stared at it confused, but her attention seemed to change quickly and she looked away. She sniffed the air and then ran towards our house. I sighed in relief, and then turned around to check on Jonathon. He stared at me in shock. He was staring directly at me as if …

"Can you see me?" I asked, surprised. He quickly jerked his head in what looked like a nod, I think. He was dumbstruck.

"I was dead. I think? What are … are you an angel?" Jonathan said really fast, shaking and putting a hand to his head. I went and put a hand on his shoulder, looking him in the eyes and chuckled. Am I an angel? Nah, no way. Right?

"I am really not sure," I said honestly. "But maybe, I guess. Now go, run. Take one of those cop cars. I'll take care of … all of this." I made the force field around us disappear … somehow.

What the hell is going on? I thought to myself.

Jonathan nodded, still obviously in shock, but seemed to shake it off and ran towards a cop car. I heard a screech and turned towards my house. I saw my mom jump into my room through the hole. How was I going to help her? I felt a presence that I recognized.

Kate? I thought, confused. What was she doing?

Come on. she said. I felt something pull on me and then everything went black.

Chapter 35

I'm … alive?

I'm alive …

So weak …

So … hungry …

KILL!!!

Wasn't I just dead?

Instincts took over—Jean Tree got up and jumped towards an Asian cop near her, knocking the gun out of his hand and brought him to the ground. She sank her teeth into the cop's neck and drank his blood. As she drank his blood, she felt herself become more aware of her surroundings and felt stronger. She drank the life out of him and then ripped her teeth from his neck and looked around. She was in front of her house. Something felt wrong though—how was she alive right now?

I felt a stabbing pain in my shoulder and looked away from my house. There were three other cops shooting at me not far down the road, trying to hurt me … rage burned through my veins …

STOP!!! KILL!!! EAT!!! is all that screamed in my head.

I jumped off the Asian cop and ran towards the other three cops, dodging the bullets they fired at me with ease. My body moved purely out of instinct, I didn't think about anything for even a second. I grabbed a large piece of glass from the ground and threw it into one cop's heart. Then I jumped onto a woman cop and sank my teeth into her neck, ripping off a piece of it. The blood … it tasted so good! It provided me with so much energy, it felt like my whole body was tingling.

I almost forgot about the last cop, but he was eager to remind me by shooting at me in the shoulder. *KILL!!!* I spat out the chunk of skin in my mouth and jumped at him, grabbed his head, and broke it. It was so easy, it felt like I had simply broken a small stick. When he fell to the ground, I picked up his arm and bit into his wrist to drink his blood. My wounds began to heal as I drank. I sucked as much as I could from him until he went dry. I then went back to the woman and bit into the wound I had already made at her neck.

What are you doing, Jean? a voice said in the back of my head. It was a very small voice, so I was able to ignore it, like a small itch. I sucked the woman dry of blood. Then went to the cop with the piece of glass in his heart and sunk my teeth into his neck.

Do you realize what you're doing? Stop! the itchy-voice said again, but louder. I hesitated and stopped drinking the man's blood. It tasted so good though …

A gun went off behind me and hit me in my back shoulder. It instantly started to heal, but it still hurt. I turned around and saw the Asian cop that I had bitten into and definitely killed a few seconds ago. How was he still alive? I didn't care—my instincts took over.

KILL!!!

I ran at him, ready to break him into pieces for not dying the first time! I jumped into the air at him, when all of a sudden, a green bubble exploded into existence around him. Unable to stop my momentum, I ran into it and fell backwards. The Asian man stood inside this green translucent bubble, looking around in awe. My anger started to boil.

A breeze went by and I smelled something else …a scent that wasn't normal human blood …

ALASTAIR!! KILL!!!! I didn't care about this stupid Asian cop anymore. Alastair did this to me! Alastair is the reason my parents were dead!!! I ran towards my house.

KILL!!!!!!!

The first thing Joshua Tree noticed as he came back to life was the smell of blood. It was gross … but also amazing. Not because he liked the smell of blood, but the fact that he smelled so much of his own blood and still lived was amazing.

A breeze went by, and it felt so nice against my cheek. Then I felt the sun warming my skin. Slowly I opened my eyes and strangely I felt like all the colors of the forest were brighter than usual. The sun was also bright in the sky, but it was only the middle of the afternoon. With everything that happened, it felt like the longest day of my life.

Pretty crappy day, too, dying and all, I thought, feeling exhausted. I tried to take a breath, but I couldn't quite get a decent one.

I looked down and—obviously kind of shocked—noticed the root Kate had stabbed me with was still plunged into my heart and connecting me to the tree behind me. It actually didn't hurt, but felt more like this intense pressure. I grabbed it and slowly pulled it out of me … now it hurt. I ripped it out from the tree behind me, out of my heart, and then out of my body. I screamed as I got the last bit of it out of me, dropping it to the ground. I fell to my knees. The hole in my chest quickly healed and the pain immediately subsided, but it left me gasping from how much it had hurt.

I stood up and touched my face, also looking at my body in general. There was a lot of blood on me that had dried into a gross crust, but all my cuts, bruises, and broken bones were healed. My gym shorts and shirt were still a mess though. I looked across from me and noticed that in the shade stood a female figure.

"Kate?" I called out, my voice sounding hoarse. "How did you bring me back? Kate?" The figure slowly walked forward out of the shade and into the sun, revealing irises that glowed purple.

"Mom?" My heart skipped a beat as I noticed all the blood on her face and arms.

A breeze blew through the air, causing the trees around us to shift.

Jean Tree smiled.

Chapter 36

Jean sprinted with her supernatural speed towards the hole in her house. When she got up to her house, she paused and looked inside the huge hole to Joshua Tree's room, assessing the situation. There—kneeling over some man with white hair that Jean didn't recognize—was Alastair. He held a knife to the man's throat, probably about to kill him.

Raged flowed through my veins—this demon murdered my parents and my husband. He was also why I was like this. I looked at the back of his neck and I felt uncontrollable hunger shiver through my being again. He smelled … different than the humans, too. Obviously, it was because he wasn't human. Come to think of it … the white haired man smelled different, too. My instincts took over.

KILL!! the monster screamed inside me.

I screeched, unable to hold my rage anymore, then jumped into the room and onto Alastair's back, biting the back of his neck. His blood tasted … AMAZING!

I didn't just taste his blood though—it was something more—something powerful! He screamed in pain and stood up, dropping his knife with a *clang* onto the ground and throwing me off his back. I slid across the room on my feet, easily keeping my balance. He turned to look at me in shock. The man with white hair quickly got up on his knees and looked at me, too. Alastair first looked shocked, then enraged, with a bit of fear in his eyes. That amused me.

"This is impossible! No human has ever survived that curse!!" Alastair yelled in shock.

"Alastair, what did you do!?" the man with white hair yelled at him. I tore my eyes off Alastair and looked at the man with white hair. I smiled, revealing my teeth to intimidate him.

"He created a monster," I said.

KILL!! I looked back at Alastair and pounced on him.

Nicholas sprang into action and tackled Jean away from Alastair. He pushed her with as much strength as he had left and surprisingly had enough strength to cause her to go flying out the hole of Joshua's room, tumbling out onto the grass in the front yard.

I heard Jean screech at me in anger as she hit the ground outside. I seemed to have hit her hard enough that she was winded and laid on the ground trying to catch her breath, but I had to act quickly. I didn't just purposely save Alastair, he just happened to get lucky. I had to stop this creature as soon as possible, and unfortunately, I might need his help. I grabbed Alastair's special knife off the ground and pointed it at him. Alastair hesitated.

"You idiot!" I yelled at him. "Trying these kinds of curses on people? Do you even fully understand what you did to her?" He simply smirked at me, but I could see a bit of worry in his black and red eyes. "You don't, do you? You tried something new, beyond your understanding. You realize how powerful you could have made her?"

"I didn't think she would survive!" he yelled back.

"Well, I just saved your life! Help me stop her!"

I heard her growl get louder as she ran towards the room and jumped in again, this time her purple irises focused on me. I swung the knife at her, but she easily ducked under my swing and jumped into my stomach.

She's so fast, I thought as she rammed me into the wall. *And strong.* She then sunk her teeth into my side and I felt the worst pain ever. She literally was sucking at my grace! My grace had already been put through enough and now she was sucking more power out of it. *I might not make it out of this one alive,* I realized in fear.

"Alastair!" I screamed at him, pleading for help. I took a quick glance at Alastair, who had a smug grin on his face, enjoying my precarious position. I tried to push Jean away from me, but she was so strong.

KATE!! Come! I'm struggling!! I mentally shouted through our connection in desperation.

Joshua Tree's wounds started to heal as Kate Iris brought him back to life. She had her hands on him and the tree, using its power to bring him back. When the process was done, she stepped back as he slowly healed.

I was proud of myself. Problem was, I still didn't feel anything for Tree. I wasn't necessarily happy he was alive again. I wish I was, but it felt more like I was proud of myself for being able to bring a person back to life. It was an accomplishment. I felt Nicholas increase our connection—he was in pain.

KATE!! Come! I'm struggling!! He screamed at me. I had to obey, I had no choice. Joshua Tree's eyes started to move under his eyelids, he'd be fine. Luckily Nicholas was too distracted to notice Joshua Tree was right in front of me being brought back to life. If he knew that he was alive, he'd just have me kill him again. I quickly jumped into the air and flew away, towards Joshua Tree's house.

Chapter 37

Alastair watched in amusement as Jean Tree bit into Nicholas' side, she seemed to be sucking him of his power. He struggled as she slowly killed him.

I *did create a monster … she's beautiful,* I thought in awe. I watched with amusement and amazement—she wasn't just a regular vampire—she was something more. I did not expect her to have actually survived that curse I infected her soul with, but I was happy she did. I had only done this curse one other time and the person died. It was a very complicated curse that I had learned … well, forever ago. Now it had finally worked.

I could use her, but I'm not sure I could control her, I thought as Nicholas continued to struggle to push her off as she hung on to him and had her teeth locked into his side, like a leech. He was dying.

I probably wouldn't be able to control her … I'll let her kill Nicholas and then try and find her later and figure her out. Right now, I need to get out of here before she's done with him and moves on to me.

Making my decision, I located the knife on the ground, which Nicholas had dropped when Jean tackled him, and made my way to the hole in the wall. I was about to fly out of the room when that little girl that Nicholas brought back from the dead came flying at me from outside, tackling me down to the ground.

She punched me in the face and grabbed the knife out of my hand, then jumped off me. It all happened so fast, I was disorientated. I heard a screech and looked up. Kate had stabbed Jean in her back. Kate then bashed Jean in the face with her fist, causing her to fall to the ground unconscious. Blood flowed out of her lower back.

"No!" I screamed. *I can't let her die—she's my creation!* I shot a dark blast at Kate, shooting her out of the room and down the hall of the house. Nicholas fell to the ground and seemed to pass out. I looked around to see if Kate had dropped the knife, but it had gone with her. I regretfully decided to leave it behind. I probably shouldn't fight that girl when she had the weapon. I picked up Jean in my arms and flew out of the room through the hole in the wall. I flew through the air, the sun slowly making its way towards the west. It was still early afternoon though.

What a long crappy day. I thought flying over the cul-de-sac and the forest with Jean in my arms. I was not even sure of where I was going, but I needed to get far away from that girl and the angel. Jean groaned in my arms in pain, her eyes closed.

"See, Jean, I just saved you. You help me, I help you," I said to her as she panted in my arms. Blood dripped out of her back; I felt for the wound. It was just above her hip on the lower right side of her back. She growled at me as I touched it. She seemed to be slowly gaining some consciousness.

"Oh, shut up, it's going to take a bit, but I can easily heal that for you." She growled louder and opened her eyes. Her purple irises focused on me, her face contorted into pure rage. She screeched, lurched forward, and bit into my neck.

I screamed in pain and dropped her.

"Ahh, you bitch!! Forget you!" I screamed as she fell towards the forest under us.

I hope she splats.

Jean screamed as she fell towards the ground, wind flipping her around. She fell into the forest, smacking and breaking some branches—and bones—along the way until she hit the ground with a *thump.*

I lay on the ground for a while in pain. Slowly, whatever just broke from that fall inside of me started to heal. That dude with the white hair had some interesting tasting blood. It provided me with enough power that my body started to heal itself quickly, so things just all *snapped* back into place.

I slowly stood up when I felt strong enough, but my lower right side flared in a bit of pain and I hesitated.

Right, that bitch stabbed me with some damn knife. For some reason, the knife wound was taking a lot longer to heal, but it slowly was. I looked around at my surroundings. My senses had fully changed because of whatever Alastair had done to me, I could *smell* and *see* almost every detail around me in this forest, it was … *amazing.*

Maybe this curse isn't such a bad thing, I thought, looking at this new world around me. I felt like I could see every detail of the world now. I smelled dried-up blood and looked at my hands, which were covered in it. Flashes of the faces of those cops came into my mind, their screams, and their fear. I actually could recall the *smell* of their fear, and the taste of their blood. Tears slowly made their way down my cheeks as I stared at my bloody hands.

What did I do? What have I become? A breeze went by and

I smelled a familiar scent. *Joshua?* I could tell it was him and I could smell … his blood. It was so strong; he obviously had lost a lot of it. I ran towards the smell, hoping he wasn't dead. I ran through the forest with this new speed of mine, trees flying by me in a blur. I found Joshua in seconds by following his scent.

I stopped and watched him in the distance. He was covered in blood and had some kind of stick stuck through his heart, which connected him to this huge tree. His body was pinned to the tree so that it had him standing up and leaning back on it.

He's dead, I thought. My heart felt like it had stopped. I could tell he was. I didn't hear his blood pumping or his breath. He was gone. My only son was gone.

The scary thing is … I didn't just feel sadness as I stared at my son's dead corpse. I felt hunger.

Joshua Tree opened his eyes.

Chapter 38

Jean watched as her son opened his eyes, oriented himself, and then slowly ripped the thick root out of his body, disconnecting himself from the tree. He screamed as he got the last bit of it out of his chest and fell to his knees.

I heard his heart instantly start beating again, when he removed the root from it, his blood now pumping throughout his body again. My mouth dropped in shock.

What the hell is happening? How did he even …

He then slowly stood up and looked around. He easily noticed me standing here in the distance.

"Kate?" He called out questioningly, his voice a little hoarse. I realized he couldn't see me here, standing in the shade.

Kate?

"How did you bring me back, Kate?" he asked.

Kate brought him back to life? How? I stepped out into the sun so that he could see me.

"Mom?"

A breeze went through the air, causing the trees to shift around us … and causing the smell of my son's dried blood scent to flow towards me even more. My instincts fought their way up as I tried to force them back down.

... KILL

I smiled, honestly happy to see him still alive. My son smiled back at me, obviously happy to see me, but I could see the question in his eyes.

He was still scared, and he was right to be. I lurched forward to kill him.

My mom's face went from smiling, to pure rage in a second. She ran at me like a lion after a deer.

"MOMMY, PLEASE, NO!" the little kid inside me yelled as she lurched after me. I was so done with my loved ones being turned against me.

She jumped into the air at me and I jumped out of the way, rolling on the ground and to my feet. Her nails ripped into the ground where I had just stood. As soon as I rolled to my feet, I ran away from her into the woods. I heard her screech in anger behind me.

I ran for my life through the forest in the direction of my house, knowing she wasn't far behind. When I heard her scream in the distance again, I looked behind me for a second and tripped. I tumbled across grass and came to a stop.

My mom burst from a clump of bushes nearby and looked around. I almost screamed, but my voice caught in my throat. She looked around … like she couldn't see me.

What the hell?

She sniffed the air, but still didn't seem to notice me, when I was only like eight feet away or something. She sniffed the air again and seemed confused, too. She ran off back towards the direction of the tree.

Whaatt the hellll? I thought again, when I noticed that my arm was missing.

WHAT THE HELL? I quickly moved it and obviously felt it still there, but when I lifted it, I noticed it was completely green—well, more like a mix of green and brown and all that. It was camouflaged to the ground. I looked at myself up and down and realized my whole body was camouflaged into my environment—yes, even my clothes.

What … the… Hell?

It kind of clicked in my head randomly.

I'm going to give you powers, Joshua Tree, I remembered God mentioning. So obviously, this was one of them. Camouflage … huh, was interesting, but weird. Apparently, even my scent must have been affected, because even if my mom couldn't see me, she should have been able to smell me, since it was obvious her smelling senses were heightened. So my body could completely disguise itself into the environment … again, interesting, but weird.

No time to ponder on this much anymore. I got up and started running again, as slowly my body and clothes went back to their normal state. I ran in between two houses and into the cul-de-sac. The front of my house looked like a war zone—cop cars and ambulances all wrecked. Surprisingly, nobody was around either. The neighbors probably ran or were hiding inside their houses after seeing what had happened. I'm sure more cops would be on their way though—probably a whole freaking army of them. I ran through the wreckage in my front yard and saw a huge hole in my house revealing my room.

"Oh, my God … " I knew that there was a hole there, but I had seen it when I was … not in reality. It was like I was practically in a dream at that time. So seeing all the destruction now was still a shock.

I walked towards it and stepped into my room through the hole. I looked around at my destroyed room, scraps of the wall on the ground. Nobody was here anymore though—I had to move. I went to my closet and grabbed my backpack. Then went to my drawer and stuffed as many clothes as I could into it. I ran to my bathroom and threw a shampoo bottle, toothpaste, my toothbrush, and deodorant into my bag.

What? I'd have to clean up eventually. I jogged back into my room.

My mom stood in the middle of it.

"Where you off to, honey?" she asked.

Chapter 39

Jean stared at her son, as he looked at her in fear from the doorway to his room. He dropped the backpack he was carrying in shock.

KILL!!!! her instincts screamed in her head. She knew this was her son. She knew it was wrong. But she didn't care. She couldn't fight who she was now. She wanted his blood, needed it. She jumped into the air at Joshua Tree.

"NO!!!" he screamed, lifting his hand into the air towards me. His irises flashed from his natural brown to glowing green. A translucent green bubble ignited into existence around him. I slammed into it and fell backwards.

This bubble again?

Joshua stared at me with his glowing green irises and his arm in front of him, focused on keeping this barrier between us.

What the hell? I thought in awe.

His face was angry, yet tears also fell down his cheeks, too.

"Go, Mom!! Leave me alone!" he yelled at me.

"Leave me alone!" Joshua Tree yelled at his mom again. She stared at him in confusion with her purple eyes.

I kept my arm lifted, somehow keeping this green translucent bubble around me. My mom jumped at the bubble again and tried to scratch at it and break it—nothing happened though. I felt her hitting it, but I was able to keep it up.

My own mother, trying to break this barrier down and kill me … rage flowed through me.

"GO AWAY, MOM!!" I screamed, forcing the bubble forward, it turned into more of a translucent green wall and flew forward, ramming into her, causing her to go flying out of the hole in my wall and out of the house. She tumbled into the front yard and quickly got up. I let the force field fade away, walking to the hole in my wall and looked out at her, as she stared back.

As she looked at me … I could finally see the pain her face. She didn't even have to say anything, but I could tell her face said, "*I'm sorry.*" She then ran away towards the cul-de-sac and into the woods—I watched her from my room as she disappeared into them.

I wiped the stupid tears from my face and looked toward the driveway, where I saw that the only car not destroyed was the van.

"You've got to be kidding me," I said to myself, the one car that wasn't working. I decided I would give the van a chance, but I had to move quickly. I jogged back through my room and grabbed my backpack. I found my keys to the van inside a drawer on my dresser and ran outside through the hole in my wall. I don't know why, but I was hopeful that the van would come through for me.

Opening the door, I jumped into the driver seat, threw my backpack into the passenger seat, put the key in the ignition and was about to turn it, when I noticed something in the rearview mirror … my eyes.

What the hell? My irises were *green* and *glowing.* As I stared at them, they slowly stopped glowing and turned back to their regular brown. But if I looked closely I could see a slight mix of green in the brown now. I sat back and shook my head in disbelief.

What is happening to me? I asked myself. I didn't have time to think about it much now, so I twisted the key.

Tick tick tick tick

"Please … "

Tick tick tick tick tick tiiiiiiiickkkkkkk

Vroooommmm

"Oh myyyy God!! Thank you!" It was actually a miracle. I shut the car door, pulled out of my driveway, and drove away from the war zone that used to be my home. As I turned onto a main road, I saw a bunch of police cars go flying by in the opposite direction, obviously towards my house.

About twenty minutes or so later, I pulled into my college's parking lot. I couldn't think of anywhere else to go. I parked the van and then sat back and sighed. I felt relieved that I got away from that place. I didn't know what time it was, but I was done. I made my way to the back of the van to lie down in what used to be my room/bed. It didn't have any blankets or pillows or anything though, so it wasn't as comfortable as it used to be.

My old home, I was back here after all these years, but completely alone this time. *No parents*, I felt a voice somewhere inside me say.

Let it out.

I started to cry. Like really cry, embarrassing kind of crying that you'd only ever do alone, and I was alone. Friends and family dead or gone in one night, so I cried—I cried for hours. I cried until the sun went down. Then slowly, I cried myself to sleep.

Chapter 40

Joshua Tree woke up the next morning in the back of his van, just as the sun made its way up. His cheeks still wet from tears—he'd even cried while he slept.

I sat up and wiped my cheeks. *No cops or anything,* I thought, kind of surprised. I almost expected to have been woke up by some cops knocking on my van, but it was quiet. *Jeez, I smell and look terrible,* I also thought, looking at the dried-up blood and crap on me. I turned to my side to go get my bag in the front of the van, but Kate was sitting next to me blocking my way, her gray eyes were angry.

She grabbed me by the throat and pushed me back down onto my back, bashing my head on the floor of the van, totally disorientating me.

"I'm going to have to kill you," she said holding me by my throat and squeezing. I wheezed, trying to get a breath, when she lessened her grip.

I was able to get a small amount of air and squeal out, "How did you find me?"

"I could sense your soul after I had brought you back from the dead."

"That makes perfect sense."

"Left a remnant of a signal, I guess you could say." Her grip around my throat tightened. "I followed the signal here. I shouldn't have brought you back from the dead, Tree. I'm going to have to kill you. I don't want to, *but I have to.*"

She squeezed harder, my head felt light from the lack of air. Then suddenly, and unbelievably, I fell through the floor of the van, hitting the pavement under it. I gasped for breath, now under the van.

Are you kidding me? Did I just fall through the van? ARE YOU KIDDING ME?

I heard the back doors of the van burst open and saw Kate's bare feet meet the pavement.

"I know you're under there," Kate called out, "but I'm going to let you live this time. It's because Nicholas is still unconscious. He has some kind of hold on me, Tree." I felt like I could almost sense the pain in her voice but I wasn't sure. She talked so coldly now. She didn't talk the way she used to at all. "Whatever he has done to me … I can't control it, especially when he's awake. Just run away and continue to run, Tree, please. The signal on your soul has faded, so I won't be able to find you easily. But if I do find you, I will kill you. I won't even think twice about it, Tree, I can't."

With that her feet left the ground and she flew away from my van. This is when I decided to do something stupid.

"Kate, wait!!" I yelled from under the van and awkwardly shimmied my way out from under it.

Kate paused in the air facing away from me; she slowly started to turn and yelled, "What did I just say, Tree! If I see you—"

"Then don't turn around, stupid! Don't look at me!" I yelled back. She stopped from turning to look at me and looked away. I forced a small laugh. "I'm a genius, right?" She just floated in the air. She was still wearing all black and those tight black yoga-like pants … gosh, I liked those pants.

"What do you want, Tree? I have to leave." Kate said impatiently. I took a breath.

"I … " We all know what I wanted to say, "I love you"—right? YES! You're right. But even after all of this … I couldn't. Yes, because I was simply scared. I was scared to love someone, especially her, and *especially* after all this. She hurt me, and that seemed to be all that she did. It's hard to love someone who intentionally and unintentionally hurt you.

There was one thing I could say that would always be true though. "I miss you … Kate. I miss you." I looked up at her hopefully, waiting for something from her. She floated up there in the sky, her hair slightly flowing in a breeze. She was a goddess, and I was down here looking up at her like a bloody peasant, praising her.

"Stay out of my way, Tree." she said coldly. With that, she flew away like a blur.

I rubbed my sore neck and hung my head down in defeat, looking at the pavement. I was hopeful, but I got what I expected.

I can't believe this is reality. This is my reality. Slowly I walked my way back to the back of the van and went inside it, closing the two big doors behind me. I made my way to the front passenger seat, threw my bag off the seat and onto the floor out of frustration, and sat down on the seat.

"SO I CAN GO THROUGH SOLID OBJECTS NOW, GOD!?!?!" I yelled out. "You know, I kind of wish you would have told me more about what type of freakin' powers you were going to give me, so that they wouldn't scare the shit out of me!!! Oh and another thing! Camouflage and force fields? Kind of close to the freakin' powers of the freaking Invisible Woman from the freaking Fantastic Four, don't you think!" I yelled. I might have lost my mind a tad. " … gosh, those movies sucked … sorry, they were OK … but not great … just frustrated." I paused, breathing hard, hoping for *something* from God. There was no response obviously.

"Psh. Can't talk to me unless I'm dead, huh? Great! That'll make it easy to 'work with you.'" I just sat in my van for a bit, breathing loudly.

I looked around towards my college and as far as I could through the window, nervous to see any cops in the parking lot. There was nothing except for some cars that probably belonged to people who were here early to open the building or whatever. I breathed a sense of relief. Half because I was relieved not to have cops here and half because it felt nice to just yell out my frustration.

Have to keep moving. What's my next move? I looked at my bloody clothes and arms. Then looked at my face in the rearview mirror, messy hair and dried-up blood on my face. I looked over at my college building again—there was still class today.

Well, I can't go to class like this … wait am I actually considering going to class as if none of this happened? It was a weird thing to consider, but something in me wanted to go do something normal. I was tired, and could just sit in my van all day, but I honestly … just didn't want to do that. I didn't want to talk to people, but I kind of just wanted to be around them.

OK, well, I have to clean up, of course. I grabbed my backpack and went to the back of the van. Opening the bag, I took out a green shirt and some black shorts.

After changing into them, I put my dirty clothes under my driver's seat. I'd have to burn them or something eventually. I cracked one of the doors in the back of the van and looked around the parking lot again, just in case. Nobody was around and the building wasn't too far away, but I had to move fast. I put my backpack around my shoulders, slipped out of the van doors and jogged towards the building. I slipped inside, running for the bathroom. Once in the bathroom, I walked to the back where there's that large handicap stall and closed the stall door behind me, locking the latch.

Jeez, luck is on my side this morning. Just made my way into my college covered in blood and no one saw. Lucky ... well, except for almost dying already this morning, but whatever—I didn't, so I guess "lucky." I took my clothes off and took out the shampoo, toothpaste, toothbrush, and deodorant from my backpack. I was surprisingly prepared for this I know—I'm good at traveling. I did it for nine years of my life, remember? I turned the faucet on and started to wet and wash my hair.

**

About an hour and a half later, after using the shampoo and basically all of the bathroom hand soap to scrub the dried blood off my body, I walked out of the bathroom pretty clean. I looked at the clock on a wall—8:45. *My Science class thing is at .... 9:30. Right.* I found a nearby chair and waited.

Once it was close to the time for class, I went and sat in my classroom. Students slowly made their way in and then eventually the teacher did, too. I sighed to myself, and pretended it was a normal day. *Tyler isn't here today ... thank you.*

Chapter 41

After class, Joshua Tree made his way outside to the front and sat at the bench he had used the other day.

I sat down in it and just thought about what the hell I was planning to do next. This was my life now, taking it moment by moment. *The cops have to be looking for me soon. They're going to want to ask someone questions. They're going to realize both my mom's body and my body aren't near the house or something.*

As I sat here and considered my next move, a girl sat next to me. At first, I kind of just ignored her, thinking she just sat here to sit here, but I could feel her eyes on me. I continued to try and ignore her, but she wouldn't look away. I could just feel her staring at me, so I turned towards her. She had dirty blonde hair, with strands of green hair going down the right side of her face. The green in her hair matched her irises, which were also green … they almost looked like they were slightly glowing … I panicked, looking away and getting ready to get up to run or something.

A breeze went by, which brought the smell of her perfume towards me, I hesitated. Something about the smell relaxed me and I recognized it. *Oh boy, it's that nice-smelling girl.*

"Hi," Nice-smelling girl finally said to me. I hesitated, and then looked back at her green eyes. They weren't glowing, I probably just hallucinated them glowing.

Joshua ... relax. I thought to myself. *Those are normal green eyes. People have green eyes. It isn't abnormal.* I probably just have been seeing too many strange eyes lately.

"Hi," I forced myself to reply back, trying to act as normal as possible, also trying to be as attractive as possible.

"You've been going here for a while?" she asked. I nodded. "OK, cool, I just moved here recently and I signed up for my classes today."

"You just got here? I had seen you the other day. I saw you ... walking and stuff." I said. *I'm so freakin awkward.*

"Yeah, I had signed up then, but I came back today to change some of my classes—I'm kind of indecisive." she said, chuckling. I forced a smile back at her. I get nervous around pretty girls, and she was really pretty.

"Oh, OK, cool, yeah, important decisions or whatever," I said, obviously being even more awkward.

Why is she talking to me?

"You want to maybe go get some food or something?" she asked, scratching her cheek. "There's a fast food place that's not far from here. About a five-minute drive or so—I'll drive us," she said, looking at me, hopeful I'd say yes, I think.

"Oh, um, my van is here and ... "

"I'll drive you back afterwards." she said, I hesitated, not sure of what to say. "I'm sorry, I don't mean to be so pushy to hang out, I just don't have many friends and you looked ... nice." She said, looking kind of embarrassed. She stared at me with those pretty green eyes, still hopeful.

Jeez ... girls.

"OK, yeah, no problem. We could go for a bit," I said.

"Sweet, thanks," she said happily, standing up off the bench. I stood up too. She started walking, but then paused, looking back at me. "Oh, what's your name by the way?" she asked.

"Oh yeah, right, my name is Joshua."

"Cool, I'm Lizzy. Nice to meet you, Joshua," she said smiling, turning to walk to her car. I followed.

"Nice to meet you, too, Lizzy," I replied.

Epilogue

Kate flew through the night sky and landed in front of the tree, landing with a *thump*. She had come from her house, where she had left Nicholas, who was still passed out. Angels never slept, but he was so weak that he was going to be out for a while, as his grace slowly repaired itself. Seemed like he was actually going to be out for a few days—his grace was extremely damaged. She was unsure of exactly how long he was going to be out. The longer the better though.

I walked up to the tree and touched Tree's dried up blood on the bark. *I did that to him.* I didn't know why I came over here at first, but now that I was here, I knew. I came back to this spot because this is where I had actually experienced … *feelings*, at least strong feelings I mean. It was like most of the time, my feelings were crammed far down inside of me, just barely making the surface to breathe. This place used to have a special place in my heart, plus I felt something before I had brought Joshua Tree back to life here, too.

I looked at the peace sign carved into the tree, covered in a bit of dried blood, too. I still couldn't recall the memory of that. I couldn't recall most of my memories now.

My memories, along with my feelings, were either gone or so far crammed away I could barely sense them—it was almost like my soul was gone. But I knew it wasn't—I could feel it more than

I ever could actually. That's how I used these new powers of mine in the first place. How ironic, I know. But something was wrong with my soul—that I knew.

I still felt the power vibrating through the tree as I touched the bark. I wasn't sure I wanted to tell anyone about this power I had discovered inside of it. I'd keep it a secret for now. In the wrong hands, this power could destroy … well, everything. I would only have to tell Nicholas, if he demanded it from me, which hopefully he'd have no reason to.

Or hopefully, he'll stay in that coma forever, I thought. When I took my hand off the tree and turned around, a girl stood there. I took the knife from my back pocket and pointed it at her.

"Funny, I actually came for that," she said.

"Who are you?" I asked her.

She smiled and said, "You don't remember me, Kate? I'm so disappointed, we were best friends." I studied her, she did seem familiar. She had dirty blonde hair, the green strands of hair that matched the green irises that almost seemed to … glow. It clicked. *Wow, a memory. Strange.*

"Lizzy."

"Nailed it," she said. She looked almost the same from when we were kids, only slightly older and taller. How did I actually remember her? Of all the memories, I remember this one? This memory was really old.

"Finally met me here at this tree—kind of late don't you think?" I said.

She laughed and said, "I'm sorry, I got kind of lost." She walked towards me. I lifted the knife a bit higher. "Look, Kate, I'm going to need that knife."

"What for?"

"To kill Jean Tree."

"Are you kidding me? You want to kill Joshua Tree's mom? How do you even know Jean Tree?"

"She's my mom," she said smiling.

"Huh? You're Tree's sister?" I asked. Lizzy chuckled.

"*Stop* laughing. This isn't funny," I said feeling irritated.

"It is kind of funny, Kate, because, well … I am Joshua Tree."

She smiled at me as her irises glowed green.

CPSIA information can be obtained
at www.ICGtesting.com
Printed in the USA
FSOW02n0541011016
25523FS

9 781614 934615